REFLEXOLOGY & REVENGE

A COZY SPA MYSTERY (BOOK 3)

JENN COWAN

JRC PRESS

Copyright © 2018 Jenn Cowan

This book is a work of fiction. Names, characters, businesses, organizations, places, events, and incidents either are the product of the author's imagination or are used fictitiously. Any resemblance to actual person's, living or dead, events, or locales is entirely coincidental.

All rights reserved. No part of this publication may be reproduced, stored in a retrieval system, or transmitted, in any form or by any means, electronic, mechanical, photocopying, recording, or otherwise, without the prior permission of author.

❀ Created with Vellum

1

"Regina, it's Autumn," I say, stepping into the cool salon. The chime above the door echoes my arrival. I shiver slightly and rub my hands up and down my arms. In this August heat, I should welcome the air conditioning, but man, Regina has this place cold.

No one's at the front counter so I make my way back to the salon floor. The smell of hair chemicals and disinfectant fill the air and I fight the urge to gag. My sandals slap against the hardwood as I tuck my hands into the front pockets of my black scrubs. I glance around taking in the new décor.

She just had it painted and wanted my opinion. I can't say I love it. It's dark red with gold splashes every few inches. The red paint makes me think of the red room in the spa. I shiver and glance over to the far wall that connects to the spa.

I remember Eddie's mother, Laura, pointing at the connecting wall, but she disappeared before I could figure out why. She's been MIA ever since. I think she's waiting for Eddie, but he's being difficult and stubborn, to say the least.

We meet a couple times a week at the library to scour Daysville newspaper archives, but so far haven't found anything to help us figure out who killed his mother and grandparents. We're currently waiting on the case files to be released. Eddie has run into a lot of red tape in securing them, which is weird. According to Eddie, there shouldn't have been any issues. I know if Eddie would just go to the spa, his mother might tell us what happened...or maybe not. Maybe she didn't see her killer. The thought of someone sneaking up behind Laura and killing her makes me shiver again. I glance over my shoulder, relief filling me when no one's there. I've felt like someone has been watching me lately.

Eddie says he's felt like someone's been watching him too. Yesterday, he was convinced someone had been in his office, but nothing was taken. He said his office smelled like motor oil and grease. I tried to get him to tell Travis, but he's not ready to go to the police with who he really is and why he moved back to Daysville. He's convinced someone in Daysville killed his mother.

I sigh and pray that's not the case. Daysville has taken a hit with the tourists this summer after all the murders. Our once safe and friendly town is now being treated like it has a contagious disease. Hopefully, Laura's killer is long gone or dead. Daysville doesn't need another killer to add to its rap sheet.

Yes, everyone who has ever committed a crime now has a public "rap sheet," compliments of the Crafty Crew. After their leader, Mrs. Walls, was murdered, they've taken it upon themselves to display these all over Daysville. Anyone with a parking ticket, speeding ticket, vandalism, or any other crime on their record has their photo, name, and crime posted on the wall of every business, lamp post and bench around town. It's totally illegal and an invasion of privacy, but the crew think it will make a killer think twice before committing another crime. Plus, people in town know who to avoid and who to watch out for. It's created quite a divide in the community and the police are trying to shut it down.

The summer has been an interesting one. A couple of high school boys spray painted the bridge in the park orange and someone else dyed the pond purple. Then there are the locals accusing each other of being the next Daysville murderer. The police are spending most of their time trying to keep the peace around town. A lot of their time is spent taking down the "rap sheets", but the old gals are tenacious and put them right back up. Daysville's quirkiness makes me smile.

Maybe I should get the Crafty Crew to talk Eddie into going to the spa. He still won't go inside. I get it, I really do. The poor guy found his mother dead in there. After seeing several dead bodies over the past few months, I can't say I blame him. If it were one of my parents, I don't think I could ever go into the place again. I've tried to convince him that maybe something will jog his memory if he goes in, but he's not buying it. I guess I could tell him his mother's ghost is haunting the red room, but I'm afraid he'll freak out or have me locked up for being delusional. He needs to see her for himself. I shake the thoughts from my mind and focus on the fact that I'm still standing in the middle of the salon alone.

"Regina? Where are you?"

Nothing.

I turn and a picture on the wall catches my eye. It's of a pretty woman with flowing brown locks covering most of her face only revealing her dark haunted-looking eyes.

Geez, Autumn, you've been reading too many paranormal cozy mysteries. Not everything is haunted...right?

I push the thought from my mind and glance around the salon. All five stations are cleaned. Not a speck of hair in sight. It's just after five and the salon closes at four on Saturdays, but Regina always stays late. The spa usually closes at four too, but I took a three forty-five walk-in reflexology client. It's not something I make a habit of, but the spa has been like a graveyard this summer.

The summer months are usually slow. Everyone's traveling or taking a vacation and with no tourists visiting us due to all the murders, we've been dead. No pun intended. We've been twiddling our thumbs around the spa so it gave Josh and me time to figure out our vacation.

Well, it's a vacation/craniosacral training. We booked it for January and it's in Florida. The spa in January is a ghost town so it's the perfect time to take a trip. We're excited to get away from the cold weather and hit the beach, not to mention add a new modality to the spa.

I sigh thinking about the beach then focus back on the fact that Regina still isn't out here talking my ear off. She should be trying to convince me how wonderful the color red is and how I should really let her dye my hair a beautiful shade of bright red. I'm always worried she'll just slip it in when she does my highlights, but so far, I still have my copper-colored locks with a hint of golden blond in them. Something she suggested when I found a few gray hairs after my thirty-fourth birthday in June. I mean I'm too young for gray hair, right? Who am I kidding? I'm six years from the big 40. I can literally hear my biological clock ticking.

My mom also keeps reminding me of that little fact and how much she would love some grandkids to spoil, especially now that her hip's healed. She still does some PT, but according to her, she's as good as new. Dad whisked her off to Italy as soon as the doctor cleared her. They're celebrating their fortieth wedding anniversary and I'm not sure they're coming back based on their text the other day. They're loving the vineyards and the food.

They make me ache for someone to spend my life with. Get married, have babies and eventually travel the world together. I know what you're thinking. Travis is ready to give me all those things, but I'm not sure he's the one for me and he hates to travel. He and I have so much history and most of it isn't good. I shake the thought from my mind and focus on finding Regina. Her car's out front and she never leaves the salon unlocked when she goes to run an errand.

"Regina?"

Silence.

"Regina, where are you?" I make my way down the tiny hallway and check the break room.

It's empty.

The bathroom's directly across the hall. I knock on the door and when I don't get an answer, I open it.

Empty.

The hairs on the back of my neck stand up and my stomach begins to churn. I just had a mango kale smoothie an hour ago so I know I'm not hungry. No, something doesn't feel right.

The light is on in the office. Maybe she's on the phone. I knock quietly on the door before pushing it open.

Empty.

Her computer monitor is on and a newspaper article is displayed on the screen. Regina's eyesight is worse than mine so her monitor is the size of a small flat screen TV and the words are in large print. Don't worry, I have an eye doctor appointment on Tuesday, but I'm not looking forward to it. Regina refuses to go, hence the ridiculous accommodations.

I lean in and scan the article. It's about a year old and features a court case Eddie won by putting away some money laundering bigwig. Why does Regina have an article about Eddie on her computer?

"Autumn?"

I gasp and spin around. "Travis. You scared the bejeebers out of me." I place a hand to my chest to try and calm my racing heart while I take him in. He's bulked up this summer if that's even possible. Josh says he's seen him at the gym almost every day. The sleeves on his pressed white shirt are rolled up and clinging to his biceps. His black pants match his black tie, which is hanging loosely around his neck. "You shouldn't sneak up on people like that."

"Like what? It's my aunt's salon. I didn't think anyone but her would be here."

"Well, she's not here."

He frowns. "What do you mean she's not here?" He glances behind me into the office. "She texted me ten minutes ago to come by the salon and she would buzz my hair." He runs a hand through his red hair, which is looking a little shaggy these days.

My fingers itch to run my hands through it. I like his hair long. In high school, he used to put his head on my lap when we'd watch a movie and I would give him a scalp massage. I always hated when summer came because Regina would buzz it for him. The summer sun is like a magnet to thick red hair. Hence the short haircut. Sigh. "I thought maybe she went to run a quick errand, but she never leaves the salon unlocked when no one is here."

"Hmm and her car's out front. Where could she have gone?"

I shrug. "Maybe she just ran to grab something to eat."

"Maybe."

Silence.

Not sure what to say, I blurt out, "She asked me to stop by to check out the new paint color."

Travis cringes and mutters, "Like we don't have enough red in our lives."

I laugh. "Regina loves red."

"That she does." His green eyes meet mine and we stare at each other for a few moments before Travis looks away and rubs the back of his neck.

I reach for the end of my copper colored braid and twirl it in my fingers. This is how it's been between us lately. Ever since the whole James debacle, we've been awkward. Tiptoeing around each other. Not really knowing what to say. At times, even avoiding each other. I'm not proud to admit I hid from him in the grocery store the other day. I just don't know what to say or how to act around him. We don't hang out or even text anymore. It's like we've gone back to how we were before April died. I hate it, but I'm not ready to date Travis and that's what he wants, so we're at a crossroads. "Well, I guess I'm going to go."

"Don't you want to tell Regina what you think of her choice of color for the salon?" He smirks, but then clears his throat and frowns.

This is so awkward. There's no way I'm going to stay here and wait for Regina...with him. "I'll just text her."

He nods and mumbles, "I wonder where she wandered off to."

"You know Regina. She probably heard a juicy bit of

gossip and ran down to the café to share it with the dinner crowd."

Travis runs a hand over his jaw. The fluorescent light highlights his five o'clock shadow. "She wouldn't leave the salon unlocked like this though and she just texted me to meet her here. It isn't like her."

"You sound an awful lot like a detective," I joke.

He shrugs. "Guilty." Then his expression turns dark. "I'm going to call her." He reaches into his pants pocket and pulls out his cell phone. When he dials her number, we hear ringing in the office. We exchange a confused look before going into the office. Travis finds her phone on the floor next to the computer. "She never goes anywhere without her cell phone." His face turns pale and matches his shirt. "I'm going to call it in."

I reach out and touch his arm before he can dial the number to the station. "Travis, I think you're overreacting. Regina's probably fine. So, she forgot her cell phone; it doesn't mean anything. Check her messages. See if you can figure out where she is."

He sighs and some color returns to his face. "You're right. With everything that's happened in Daysville over the past six months, I'm quick to think the worst."

"I know," I whisper, feeling slightly guilty I've solved the last two big cases in town. Supposedly, Travis is taking some heat for it at the station. Maybe that has something to do with him keeping his distance these days. If we were mature adults, we would talk it out, but it's like we're in high school all over again. I shake our problems from my mind and focus on Travis. He's staring at the screen and his hands are shaking.

"What? Did she figure out who dyed the lake purple?" A couple boys fessed up to painting the bridge, but insisted they didn't dye the lake. Regina has been on the mission to find out who did. The poor swans are still a light shade of lavender.

He shakes his head and almost drops the phone.

I snatch it from his hand. "Travis, what is it?" I ask, then glance at the screen. My heart begins to beat faster in my chest and my palms go sweaty. "Wh-Who is this from?"

"No clue."

I read the text aloud, *"If I go down, you do too."* I glance up at Travis, who is cemented in place like a statue. "Is Regina mixed up in something?"

"No clue."

I let out an exasperated breath. "Can you say something else?"

He blinks and grabs the phone from my hand. "I have to go." He moves around the desk and tries to brush past me.

I reach out and grab his arm. "Travis."

He turns and looks down at my hand as if it were a snake. "Let go, Autumn," he hisses, his voice like venom.

I let his words roll off me and tighten my grip. "Travis, talk to me. What's going on?"

A flash of pain registers on across his face before he straightens and meets my eyes. "I don't know, Autumn, but I plan to find out. Will you lock up?" He rips his arm from my grasp and stomps out of the salon.

I gape after him. Who was that? It certainly wasn't the Travis I know. Something is going on and I think Travis knows more than he's letting on.

2

I shift in the middle of the pew. These wooden pews are not good for anyone's back. At least this time I'm not here for a funeral, which means I'm not wearing black either. Nope, it's just Sunday services and thankfully, I'm wearing a blue sundress with my hair in a braid to one side and my favorite tan strappy sandals. Josh, on the other hand, is wearing black. His short sleeve polo shirt is black and clings to his biceps. His shiny dress shoes are also black. The only piece of clothing that's not black is his pants, which are khaki. His dark hair is spiked up with gel and has a messy look to it. Several of the single ladies keep glancing over at him. I refrain from rolling my eyes and focus back on the sermon.

Preacher John finishes it then gives his final blessing before Violet begins to play the piano. Everyone files out of the pews and starts talking about Regina's disappearance. Regina's petite brunette receptionist, Amy, is sniffling by the door. I overhear her tell the Crafty Crew ladies that she left around four fifteen, and Regina was singing along to the radio and sweeping the floor. She didn't appear to be upset about anything. That leaves about a forty-five-minute window from the time Amy left to when I headed over to the spa. Did someone take her or did she leave willingly?

I think back to the text message Regina got and try to remember the time. Shoot. I wish I would have paid more attention. The text was unnerving, to say the least. *If I go down, so do you.* What did Regina do?

Josh places a hand on the small of my back and guides me out the back door. I smile at Preacher John, who is holding the door open for everyone. He reaches out and shakes my hand. "Good morning, Autumn. Some heat, huh?"

"Stifling," I respond, already beginning to sweat. It's ten a.m. and the bank temperature read eighty-six when we came into the church at nine. I'm sure the gauge is up ten degrees by now.

"Have you heard anything from Travis about Regina?"

I shake my head. My texts have gone unanswered. The captain won't let Travis file a missing person's report for twenty-four hours so I'm sure Travis is livid. I went over to his house last night, but Cat said he was still at the station. She was a mess. Her green eyes were red and puffy and her short red hair was sticking to her freckled face. A sight that reminded me of how she looked when she lost her mother. I offered to stay with her or have her stay at my house since she usually stays with Regina when Travis is working. She politely declined, saying she already made arrangements to stay with a friend. I told her to call or text me anytime. So far, I've gotten several texts and one phone call from her, but nothing from her father.

Preacher John squeezes my hand as if he knows my mind is elsewhere. "Well, if you hear anything please let us know. We're all very worried and are praying for her safe return." He releases my hand and smiles, but it doesn't reach his brown eyes.

"I will," I say and move out of the way so the Crafty Crew can fuss over the preacher. He lost his wife to cancer about a year ago and they've been watching over him ever since. I think he has a little crush on Regina because he blushes every time he sees her, but she's adamant she could never be a preacher's wife.

Regina's never been married. Told me she was in love once, but when Travis's parents died, she took over caring for him and he became her world. I admire her for everything she's done for Travis but always wondered what happened to her lost love. Could he be the one texting her? If so, why would he be threatening her? Were they some sort of Bonnie and Clyde couple?

The car accident was almost thirty years ago. Travis was in kindergarten...or was it first grade? It's hard to remember that far back. Maybe I need to do some more research. I glance over at the Crafty Crew ladies and know they'll tell me everything I need to know, but I'm not sure that's the best route. They love to gossip and I don't want them spreading stuff about Regina, especially if it's just a theory.

"Diner?"

I jerk at Josh's words. I kind of forgot he was standing next to me. "I think I'm going to head over to the library."

"The library? Again?" He sighs. Josh has been very vocal about all the time I've been spending with Eddie at the library. He even went so far as to ask me if we were dating. Something I guess everyone in town is wondering even though Violet has been on several dates with Eddie over the past few weeks. "Beverly doesn't even open until eleven," he adds.

Shoot. It's Sunday. Obviously, I'm standing in the church

parking lot. I'm zoning out, thinking about Regina while everyone else is heading to their cars or walking across the street to the diner. Maybe I'll find out some information at the diner. "The diner sounds good." I link my arm in his and let him lead me toward the diner.

Before we reach it, I spot a familiar silver Mercedes pulling into the church parking lot. Eddie gets out and buttons up his gray suit coat. It's almost a hundred degrees outside and Eddie refuses to go casual to church. Always dressed in an expensive suit and tie with his brown hair parted to one side. His brown eyes scan the parking lot and land on me. He motions for me to join him.

"Save me a seat." I let go of Josh's arm.

"Save you a seat? What do you mean?" Josh frowns at me.

"I need to talk to Eddie."

"Eddie?" He glances over to where Eddie is standing next to his car and scowls.

I follow his gaze and notice that Violet has joined him. She flips her dark hair over her shoulder as she laughs at something he says. She's dressed in a knee-length floral dress. Gone are the long high neck dresses and in their place, cute sundresses. She has even started wearing some make-up.

Since Gus is rehab for the second time, Violet has really come out of her shell. She found a nice one bedroom apartment on the other side of town from her childhood home and seems to be enjoying her new life.

I pat his arm. "I won't be long. Maybe Eddie has some news about Regina."

Josh mumbles something I can't hear and stomps off toward the diner.

I stare after him, hoping he'll turn around, but when he doesn't, I sigh and head toward Eddie.

"Good morning, Eddie." I smile at him and nod to Violet. "Violet, beautiful playing this morning."

Eddie flashes me a genuine smile while Violet gives me a tight one.

"Autumn." She eyes me suspiciously then turns back to Eddie. "Ready to go inside, honey."

Eddie cringes slightly at the name, but I don't think Violet saw it. "I need to chat with Autumn for a minute."

Violet's cheeks flush and I don't think she's blushing. "I could really use your help putting away all the hymnals before the next service."

"I'll be in shortly. I just have a few questions for Autumn about a case."

"Right. The 'case' you've been working on at the library several times a week." She shoots me a glare then turns back to Eddie and asks sweetly, "What 'case' is this again?"

He clears his throat before saying, "It's confidential." He gestures to the door. "Give me a couple minutes, please."

Violet completely ignores me and gives Eddie a peck on the cheek. "I'll see you inside." Then she takes off to the church in a huff.

Eddie rubs the back of his neck. "Sorry about that. She's kind of clingy."

I smile and stifle a snort. Violet has gone from the shy timid girl to a possessive mean girl in the span of one summer. Maybe being poisoned in the spring affected her more than anyone realized. "What did you want to talk to me about?"

"Regina. I found something."

"What?"

"She was friends with my mom."

"Wh-what do you mean?"

"I was going through some photo albums and found one of Regina and my mom. It looks like they graduated from the same beautician school. Then I found another one of Regina and my parents."

"Was there anyone else in the photo?"

"No, why?"

I shrug. "No reason."

"Autumn, if you have something to tell me. Tell me."

I sigh. "Have you talked to Travis?"

Eddie shakes his head. His face etched with worry. "I've tried. He won't return my calls. Everyone at the station says he's holed himself up in his office and won't talk to anyone."

I bite my lip. That doesn't sound like Travis. He's hiding something. Probably trying to protect Regina. But from what?

"Autumn?"

"Regina got a text yesterday. The number was blocked."

"What did it say?"

"*If I go down, so do you.*"

"Go down? For what?"

"No clue." Sheesh, now I sound like Travis.

Eddie leans against his car and doesn't say anything. He appears to be deep in thought.

People are parking their cars and sending us curious looks as they go inside the church. I shift back and forth on my sandals. I don't need anyone spreading any more rumors about the new PA and me. Violet may murder me and who knows what Travis will do with all this other pressure on his plate. Although he's been keeping his distance so maybe he won't care. I take a deep breath and try to ignore the stares and whispers, but it doesn't work. "Eddie, you probably need to get inside."

He snaps out of his trance and sees me looking around. "Right. Church. Meet you at the library around noon?"

"Um." I glance around again. "Maybe we shouldn't."

His brows scrunch together. "Why not? We're just doing research."

"I know, but no one else does."

"Yes, they do. I've told them."

My eyes go wide. "You've been talking about us?"

He cocks his head to the side. "Is that a problem? I'm just setting the record straight."

I sigh, not sure how to explain the inner workings of a small town to a city slicker so I just nod my head. "I'll see you at noon."

"Great." Then he pauses and says, "How about one? I almost forgot I'm taking Violet out to lunch after the eleven o'clock service."

"Will Violet be joining us?"

He frowns. "Um, I don't think so. Why?"

I snort. "If you haven't noticed she doesn't like us talking and she especially hates us spending time together."

Eddie waves it off. "Let me deal with Violet."

I shrug and mutter, "It's your funeral."

He smirks. "I'll see you at 1 p.m." Then he waves before hurrying inside the church.

I turn and head toward the café. A screech of tires has me turning back around and catching a glimpse of red.

Regina's car.

3

It's the only red car in town. I squint to see the driver, but it whips by in a flash. Shoot. I fumble with the clasp on my purse and feel around for my phone. I quickly dial Travis's number and of course, he sends me to voicemail. I hurry down the sidewalk in time to see the car make a left down main street. I type out a text and send it as I continue to try and run down the street in these super cute, but totally not good for my feet sandals. When I make it to the end of the street the car's disappeared and my phone starts to ring. Travis. "About time."

He ignores my comment. "Where is it?"

"Just turned left onto Main Street. I'm on the corner of Main and Plum. It's gone."

"Gone. How could you lose it?"

"Excuse me? I'm in a sundress and three inch strappy sandals. You expect me to chase a red mustang through town in this outfit?"

He mumbles something I can't make out then hangs up on me.

I clench my jaw and refrain from running down to the

station and giving him a piece of my mind. What's his deal? I stomp back to the café and pull open the door. Just as I'm about to go inside there's a commotion at the church. People are running out into the parking lot and screaming.

Josh comes up behind me and asks, "What's going on?"

"No clue." Sheesh, I've got to quit saying that. I hurry down the steps and spot Violet. I'm not sure she'll talk to me, but I take my chances. "What's going on?"

"There's a bomb in the church."

"What? How do you know?"

"Eddie got a text."

I glance around. "Where's Eddie?"

"Looking for the bomb."

"What?! Why? He should let the police handle it."

"The text said the bomb had some information about his mother's killer on it."

My head starts to pound and my heart takes off at lighting speed in my chest. "On the bomb. Did the text say where the bomb was?"

"In the basement."

My gut tells me it isn't in the basement. It's a trap. Sirens sound in the distance. "We have to get Eddie out of there. Josh, tell him it's not in the basement."

He doesn't question me or hesitate as he takes off sprinting toward the basement steps.

Violet's chewing on her thumb nail and staring after him. I glance around and know this is my chance to find the bomb.

If I were a bomb, where would I be?

What if there isn't even a bomb? If there is, could Regina have planted the bomb? I shake the thoughts from my mind. She doesn't know anything about bombs, right? Everything I know about Regina is beginning to get jumbled in my mind. I'm actually suspecting her of doing something awful...like killing Eddie's mother or being a part of it. I focus back on the church.

The bomber sent Eddie to the basement. So, the bomb is probably the furthest away from the basement so when he realizes it's not there it will go off before he can get out. Was it planted to scare him or...kill him?

I glance up. The bell tower. It's the furthest away from the basement and when the bomb goes off, the bell and stones will rain down right in front of the basement steps. Killing or trapping Eddie. I gulp and hurry toward the bell tower steps.

The metal stairs run up along the side of the church. I look over my shoulder to see if anyone is watching me, but everyone is staring at the basement steps. Two police cruisers pull up, but not Travis. He must be looking for Regina's car. I'm not sure what I'm going to find at the top of the steps, but I know I have to try. My heart is thumping like crazy and my palms keep slipping off the metal handrail. The stairs are rickety and shake with each step. I feel like I'm walking to my death. I pray it's not a phone triggered bomb. You know the ones where someone calls it and it goes off or the one where someone presses a button and it goes off. Please don't let it be one of those.

I glance back down at the parking lot. I'm really high up. Everyone looks so small. I sway slightly. Did I mention I hate heights? No? Well, I do. Why do you have to be hero, Autumn? You could have just told the police your suspicions. They would have believed you. You have solved two cases in this town over the past six months. Surely, I have credibility by now, right? I can't risk it. I'm almost to the top anyway so I keep going.

When I reach the bell tower. The large bell sways

slightly in the wind. I glance toward the bank clock to see if it's going to ring soon. Shoot, it's too far. I squint and sigh. Too bad my eye appointment wasn't last Tuesday.

I look around the platform and don't see anything suspicious. Huh? Maybe I was wrong. I turn to start back down the stairs when something blinking catches my eye. I bend down and look inside the bell. Well, isn't that just great.

The bomb is taped to the inside of the bell. Thankfully, it's on a timer although there's only a minute left. I run to the edge of the tower and wave my arms. "Up here! The bomb's up here!" No one even looks up at me. Wonderful. Now, what?

I fumble with my phone and call Josh.

"Autumn? The bomb's not here. Eddie won't leave. He thinks it's here."

"Josh."

"I tried to tell him, but he won't listen."

"Josh!"

"Autumn?"

"The bomb's in the bell tower. You need to get out of there now."

"What?! Where are you?" He pauses. "Autumn. You better be in the parking lot when I get out of here."

"Send the police up and hurry. There's only like 45 seconds left."

I hear mumbling and rustling. I spot the officers rushing toward the stairs. I know it's time to move. Time to get down from the tower, but I'm frozen.

Officer Buckler steps up next to me. I can't see his face. He's decked out in protective gear. He's Daysville's bomb specialist. "Autumn?"

I point to the bell.

He bends down and checks the timer. "You need to get down. Quickly."

"Can you stop it?"

He ignores me and focuses on the bomb, which is what he should do.

Another officer in protective gear holds out a hand to me and I follow him down the stairs. I'm counting the whole time as we make our way to the café. Everyone has been moved from the church parking lot to the café parking lot to ensure no one is hit by any potential flying debris.

Josh scoops me into a hug and squeezes so tight I can barely breathe.

"Josh," I cough out.

He puts me down, but keeps an arm firmly around my shoulder. "Don't do that to me."

I tuck a strand of loose hair behind my ear and whisper, "I'm sorry. I had to find the bomb."

He nods, but I can tell he's upset.

My heart is pounding as the clock dwindles down. Only five seconds left. I spot Eddie staring at the church. His jaw is set and his eyes are a blaze. It doesn't take a psychologist to see the guy's furious. His eyes meet mine and he cocks his head. I know what he's asking. I shake my head. There wasn't any information about his mother's killer on the bomb. It was a total set up, but why?

Eddie just told me he's been "setting the record" straight about all the time we're spending in the library so maybe someone thinks we've found something or is it something unrelated to his mother and grandparents' deaths? My gut tells me it's related, but how?

Time's up.

4

I hold my breath and wait.

Nothing.

The officers make their way down the stairs. Several other officers come out of the church and town hall to ensure there aren't any more bombs. Looks like it was just one. Officer Buckler is holding the bomb in his hands. He disappears into a vehicle and it takes off toward the station. Once his vehicle disappears from sight, we get the all clear to go home. More police cruisers show up to question and escort everyone to their cars. I give my statement quickly and they let me go with a heads up they may call me for more information later. I nod and walk back toward Josh, who also just finished up being questioned.

He pushes himself off the café rail. "Hungry?"

I shake my head. "I think I just want to go home and lie down."

"I ordered you oatmeal. I'll have them pack it up for you and settle the bill."

I smile and watch as he heads inside the café.

"Was there anything on the bomb?"

I jump and find Eddie behind me.

"Sorry, didn't mean to scare you." He runs a hand through his hair. Violet's plastered to his side. Gripping his bicep like it's a life preserver. Her brown eyes are wide and she looks like a deer in headlights. She's staring at the church. I wonder if she's waiting for it to blow up.

I wave off his apology. "There wasn't anything on the bomb." I glance around and lower my voice since several people are still standing in the parking lot. I'm not sure if they're afraid to move or just waiting to get questioned and gossip about the bomb. "The bomb must have been a trap. If it went off, you would have been trapped or worse."

He clenches his jaw. "I know." Then his eyes soften. "Thanks for giving me the heads up and for finding the bomb. You saved my life."

His words hang heavy in the air. I gulp, pushing down the lump forming in my throat. Eddie could have died and Josh too. Tears threaten to fall and I blink them away. There has been so much loss in Daysville over the past few months. Maybe it's all starting to catch up to me.

Eddie gives me a sympathetic smile before saying, "I was just hoping for something about my mother's case. It's been cold for so long and I thought if I came back, I could solve it. Bring her killer to justice. For her. For my grandparents. For me. Someone obviously thinks I know more than I do."

"Or they don't want you digging into the case anymore."

"Hmm." Eddie glances down at Violet. "I better get her home. They canceled services while the police investigate further. Still up for meeting me later?

My stomach churns and I feel like someone is watching us. "Are you sure you want to keep looking into this?"

His face is stoic as he replies, "Absolutely." Then he studies me. "Are you sure you still want to help me? It's one thing to put myself in harm's way, it's another to ask you to risk your life."

I swallow the bile rising in my throat. The thought of being blown to bits is not on my bucket list, but I can't let Laura's killer get away. They need to be brought to justice… no matter who they are. My thoughts drift to Regina before I shake them away and say, "I'm in."

"You sure?"

I nod.

He bites his lower lip and whispers, "If at any time you want out just say so. No hard feelings. I promise."

I smile. "I'm in it till we catch the killer."

He grins and reaches out like he wants to squeeze my hand, but glances down at Violet and pulls his hand back then says, "Thanks, Autumn. You don't know how much this means to me."

Before I answer, an officer calls out to Eddie and waves for him to join them.

"I'll text when I'm on my way. One o'clock still work?"

"Sounds good." I watch him untangle himself from Violet, who seems completely shell-shocked. She didn't even protest when Eddie talked about meeting me. The poor thing has been through a lot lately.

"Ready to go?"

I jump again. I'm not usually this skittish.

"Sorry." Josh gives me a sheepish look.

"It's fine."

He frowns. "You sure? You haven't been yourself lately."

I make a face. "What do you mean?"

"You just seem kind of withdrawn and distant."

I scoff and start walking toward my Jeep. "I'm fine. Just tired of this heat. It makes me grumpy, you know that."

"You sure it doesn't have anything to do with Travis dating Allison Cole?"

I whip around and gape at him. "Travis is dating Allison?"

Josh's jaw drops and his eyes go wide. "I thought you knew."

Tears threaten to spill from my eyes, but I blink them back and hurry to the Jeep. Once inside, I take a few deep breaths. How did I not know this? It's Daysville. Everyone knows everything...apparently, I don't. "How long?" I whisper when Josh slides in next to me and squeezes my hand.

"They went to the Fourth of July picnic together and have been dating ever since. Regina set it up. Thought it would be good for Travis to get back in the game since you weren't interested in dating him."

I don't respond because this is my fault. I told him I wasn't ready to date him. I can't expect him to wait on me forever while I figure things out. I envision Travis and Allison together. Allison with her silky dark red hair and creamy complexion. She loves Pilates and yoga and it shows. She's kind of ditzy, but sweet and loves doing hair. She's the perfect fit to take over Regina's salon when and if she ever decides to retire. Maybe Regina wants to keep the salon in the family. The thought of Travis and Allison getting married and having babies together makes my stomach roll.

"You've been spending all summer at the library with Eddie. I guess Travis just assumed you were dating him."

"We're not dating," I growl.

Josh holds up his hands. "I know. Just giving my two cents on the matter."

I roll my eyes.

"Autumn." He pauses and rubs a hand over his face.

"What?"

He sighs then asks, "Why are you spending so much time with Eddie? If you're not dating, why all the trips to the library? I know you said it's confidential, but I mean, I'm your best friend. You can tell me anything and it won't leave this car."

I open my mouth to tell him what I've been telling him all summer. Eddie is working on a case and asked for my help. It's confidential and I can't share the details, but now it seems kind of silly. Josh is my best friend and I've been shutting him out. Just like I shut out Travis when he questioned me on the case, and even offered his services. Now, Travis is dating someone else and Josh thinks I don't trust him. Way to go, Autumn. I bite my lip not even knowing where to start so I decide to just show him. "Go to the spa."

5

"Well, we're here." Josh shuts off the Jeep and faces me.

I push open the passenger side door and hop out. "Inside. I need to show you."

"Show me what?" He follows me to the back door and unlocks it before holding it open for me.

"This way." I flip on a couple overhead lights as I make my way to the red room.

"Autumn, why are we here? What does the spa have to do with Eddie?"

I don't answer him as I walk into the red room. It's abnormally cold. Laura must be waiting for me.

Josh steps in next to me and the door slams shut behind him.

Shoot. I forgot to grab something to prop open the door. Surely, Laura won't trap us in here, right?

"Is the air conditioner broken? It's freezing." Josh rubs his hands up and down his arms.

I take a deep breath and see it on the exhale. I turn to Josh and say, "Are you ready?"

He frowns and asks, "Ready for what?"

"Laura."

"Who's Laura?"

"Eddie's mom."

Josh blinks at me, studying me for a moment then it clicks and his eyes go wide. "You mean...her gh-ghost?"

I nod.

"Autumn quit messing with me." He bumps my arm and smirks. "Very funny. If you don't want to tell me about what you and Eddie are up to you could just tell me to mind my own business. You don't have to make up a story about seeing his mother's gh-." He quits talking when her shimmery image appears. She's still beautiful in her ghostly form with her long flowing dark hair and dark eyes. Josh clamps a hand down on my arm and his jaw drops open. "It's a gh-ghost."

"Yes, it is."

He turns to look at me for a second and then focuses back on Laura. "What does she want?"

I sigh. "She wants Eddie to come visit her, but he won't."

"Why not?"

"He found her...here."

He scrunches his eyebrows and cocks his head at me. "What do you mean?"

"I mean he f-o-u-n-d her." I'm trying to be sensitive to Laura by not blurting out that Eddie found her dead body.

Josh continues to stare at me like I'm speaking a foreign language.

I roll my eyes and mouth, "Her body."

His mouth goes into an O and he nods before turning back to Laura.

I focus on Laura and smile.

She smiles back.

"This is Josh." I gesture to him.

She nods.

"Eddie and I are working on your case, but we're not finding anything."

She looks confused for a moment. Then I remember Eddie changed his name. "I mean Walter and I are working on your case."

Her smile goes wider before she frowns and points to the wall separating the spa from the salon.

I step closer to her and look at the wall. It's painted red, but I don't see anything except a wall. "I don't understand." I turn to look at her only to find she's disappeared. "Laura? Please don't go. We want to help you." I wait. The room warms slightly and the door opens. Guess that means she's done talking to me. I shake my head in frustration and move toward the door.

Josh follows me. "Do you think I scared her off?"

I shake my head.

"I can't believe we saw a ghost. I never thought I would ever see one. It's kind of cool." He pauses from his excitement and asks, "So, you've been helping Eddie research his mother's murder? Why didn't you just tell me? I would have helped."

I shrug. "Eddie didn't want anyone to know. He moved to town to solve her case, but doesn't want word to get out that he used to be Walter Smoot."

Josh's mouth falls open. "Wasn't he the boy in kindergarten who found his mother..." His voice trails off as everything sinks in. "Eddie Bell is Walter Smoot. How?"

"He was adopted after his grandparents were murdered. They used his middle name, Edward and he took his adoptive parents' last name."

Josh nods but doesn't say anything. He seems to be processing all this information.

I give him a minute and wonder if Travis knows Eddie's true identity. Then my mind goes to Travis and Allison and I quit thinking about him.

Josh interrupts my thoughts. "So, Eddie thinks someone in Daysville killed his mother?"

"And his grandparents. Possibly his father."

Josh's head jerks back. "Someone killed his whole family?"

"Maybe. It's a hunch his father's car accident wasn't really an accident." I glance back at the wall. Before I can say anything else a blast of cold air hits me and a vision plays like a movie in my mind.

Laura is cowering against a white wall. Her dark hair falling in front of her face as tears fall down her cheeks. "I don't know where it is. Please. Don't hurt me. I have a son," she cries.

I hear a gun cock behind her. A shadow is cast on the wall from the afternoon sun. The shadow is wearing a ball cap but doesn't say anything.

"Please. I'll keep looking," Laura begs.

The gun goes off.

I scream and fall forward, clutching my chest. It burns like I spilled something hot on it. My breathing is heavy and my heart feels ready to burst.

"Autumn, what's wrong?" Josh drops down next to me on the floor and puts a hand on my back. "Are you having a panic attack?"

I shake my head because I can't find my voice. Honestly, I feel like I've been shot. I take a few deep breaths and try to slow my racing heart. My whole body is shaking and my teeth begin to chatter.

"Autumn, talk to me?"

Reflexology & Revenge

"I-I'm o-ok," I say, through chattering teeth.

Josh pulls an old blanket off a shelf and wraps it around my shoulder. "Let's get you out of here. Can you stand?"

I try, but my legs give out. He scoops me up into his arms and takes me from the red room. I rest my head on his chest and listen to his heart. It's soothing and finally, my breathing slows and the burning in my chest subsides. Hot air hits me and I squint in the bright sun. "Wh-where are we going?"

"Home."

I don't object because lying in my own bed sounds incredible right now. Josh unlocks the Jeep and settles me into the passenger seat. When he's walking around to the driver's side, my phone starts to ring. I grab my purse, which I left in the car and pull out my phone. Eddie. I glance at the clock. It's only eleven thirty. Sheesh, it seems later than that with everything that's happened this morning. "Hello."

"Autumn, where are you?" he asks, breathing hard like he's been running.

"The spa. Why?"

"Someone broke into my house."

6

"We need to get home. Someone broke into Eddie's house."

Josh frowns, pulls onto Main Street and steps on the gas.

I check my phone. Twenty missed calls. Most of them are from Eddie. A few from Nikki and two from Cat. I shoot a text off to Nikki, who responds by telling me about the break-in at Eddie's then tells me she won two tickets to Luke Bryan's Farm Tour in Villsboro on Friday and I'm going with her since she and Bobby are taking some space. Guess I'm not the only one dealing with man problems. I dial Cat's number, but it goes straight to voicemail. I leave a message and look out the windshield.

As we pull into our cul-de-sac, Josh and I exchange a look. The street's filled with people and police cars. Barricades have been placed at the end of Eddie's driveway blocking the crowd from getting any closer. People move to the side to allow Josh to park in my driveway. I get out and take in the scene.

Police lights are flashing in front of the house next door. Yes, Eddie is our new neighbor. He moved in the first of June. His two-story Tudor style home looks out of place compared to the rest of the ranch-style houses on the block, but the former owners the Whiteman's were obsessed with the style and insisted on building it. Eddie's not crazy about the style, but it was the only house for sale in the entire town.

Travis makes eye contact with me and nods his head before turning back to the officer he was talking to. He's wearing a wrinkled white shirt with the sleeves rolled up to his elbows and dark pants that appear to have just come out of the dryer as a dryer sheet is clinging to the cuff around his ankle.

Eddie steps out onto the front stoop. He's still wearing his suit from church. He spots me and strides over. Before he reaches us, a shriek comes from the bottom of his driveway and someone practically barrels him over.

"I came as soon as I heard," Violet gushes, letting him go enough to look him over to be sure he's uninjured. "Why didn't you call me?"

He opens his mouth then closes it. His brown eyes are blank and he's floundering.

I decide to rescue him. "I'm sure he didn't want to worry you after the bomb incident."

Violet turns to take me in. Her brown eyes flashing with annoyance as she gives me a closed-lipped smile. "Well, you shouldn't worry about that, Eddie." She faces him and gives his hand a squeeze. "What happened?"

"I heard a noise in my study when I walked in after dropping you off and found someone rifling through my file cabinet. They took off when they saw me."

"Did you see their face?"

Eddie shakes his head.

I frown and the hairs on the back of my neck stand up, causing me to shiver.

"Are you cold?" Josh asks, putting an arm around me. "It's so muggy out, but after what happened at the spa…" He glances at Eddie, who tenses at the mention of the spa.

I glance behind me. I can't shake the feeling someone is watching us. "I'm fine."

Travis clears his throat and eyes Josh's arm around me before turning to Eddie. "You stated they were dressed in all black, correct?"

Eddie nods.

"There are no signs of forced entry and you're positive nothing's missing?"

"Not that I know of."

Travis checks his iPad and taps something in it. "I'm going to check inside with the guys to see if they found anything. I'll be right back," he glances at me quickly before hurrying inside.

We stand quietly for a few minutes while we watch the police move in and out of Eddie's house.

My mind is racing with scenarios. One being Regina planting the bomb at the church then racing over here to dig into Eddie's files to see if he has any information about his mother's case in them. "Did you notice anything particular about the intruder?"

"Trying to play detective again, Autumn?" Travis asks from behind Eddie. His green eyes are dark and narrowed.

I give him my best toothy grin and say sweetly, "Just being neighborly. Want to know who or what to watch out for in case they decide to come back."

Travis's brows scrunch together. "There's no sign of

forced entry. Nothing's missing. At best, someone is just trying to scare Mr. Bell. Why? I'm not sure." He studies Eddie. "Anything you want to share? Maybe why you and Autumn have been spending so much time at the library...t-o-g-e-t-h-e-r," He draws out.

Eddie clenches his jaw and glares at Travis. "What I do in my free time, with my friends, is none of your concern, Detective."

Travis snorts. "I didn't realize you and Miss Fisher were such good friends."

Eddie flexes his fists and opens his mouth to respond, but I cut him off.

"Should I be concerned about someone breaking in?" I ask, trying to steer the conversation to safer territory.

Travis turns from Eddie and shakes his head at me. "I don't think you have to worry about anyone breaking into your house, Autumn." Then he pauses and adds, "On that note, did you ever call the home security company to get a system installed?"

"No, it's Daysville. The friendliest and safest town in Missouri."

Travis scoffs. "It was the friendliest and safest town in Missouri. You of all people know this past year has lost us that title. You need to call them. I don't want to work any more cases at your home or have you find any more dead bodies in your kitchen." His voice softens and so do his eyes. "Promise me you will call them."

I sigh and nod.

Travis studies me like he's not sure I'll actually follow through and call them. He opens his mouth to say something when an officer calls him over to the front door. He turns and jogs over to him. Several other officers are heading toward their vehicles.

"Looks like they're clearing out," Eddie mumbles, looking slightly annoyed and somewhat concerned.

"Want to come over to my house?" I offer.

His eyebrows shoot to his hairline. "Really?"

Violet huffs next to him. "You can come to my apartment, Eddie."

I smile at her. "You can come too, Violet. I can make us all lunch. It's almost noon."

Josh gives me a look like I'm crazy. After my episode at the spa, I'm sure he's going to be fussing over me all day. He's so overprotective.

Eddie runs a hand over the back of his neck and glances at Violet. "We don't want to put you out."

I rub the spot on my chest. The place where the bullet exited Laura's chest. I know she would want me to look after her son so I force a smile and say, "It's no trouble."

Violet mumbles a thank you.

Eddie bites his lower lip and glances back at his house. "Let me finish up with Detective Mills then lock up and I'll be right over."

"We'll wait for you."

He grins and nods before hurrying over to Travis.

Josh nudges me with his elbow and motions for me to step away from Violet. We do so without appearing too obvious since she's watching Eddie like a hawk zeroing in on its dinner. "What are you doing?" He whisper-yells.

I balk at him. "What do you mean?"

"Why are you inviting them over? You collapsed at the spa. You need to rest."

"I'm fine."

Josh scoffs. "I don't believe you."

I attempt my best smile and hope the sun is making my cheeks pink. "Really. I just got a little light headed." Shoot,

I'm lying to my best friend again. Maybe I should tell him the truth. "Actually..." I don't get to finish telling him because I spot something in the woods between Eddie's house and mine. I gasp and before I can warn Josh or anyone else, a gun goes off.

7

Travis's passenger side window of his SUV explodes and glass sprays all over the street. Josh drags me to the ground with him then practically covers me with his body. I lift my head enough to see Travis push Eddie into the house then duck behind a pillar with his gun pointed toward the sound of the gunshot. Only a couple officers are still here and they're taking cover behind their SUV. People on the street are screaming and running for cover. Most of them are just fleeing down the street, probably heading for their homes

Another gunshot sounds on the back side of Eddie's house and I hear glass break inside. Three more shots and glass continues to shatter with each shot. My heart is hammering in my chest. I don't see Eddie. He's inside the house. I clamp down on my cheek to keep from crying out to him. Violet is whimpering and saying Eddie's name over and over beside us while Josh tells her to stay down. Is this why Laura showed me how she died? Is Eddie going to die?

The shots finally stop probably because there are no

more windows in the back of the house. It's eerily quiet. No one moves.

Travis peeks out from behind the pillar and his eyes meet mine. He mouths, "Are you okay?"

I nod.

He gives a curt nod back then holds up a hand for me to stay put. I hear a diesel engine start up a street over and Travis breaks eye contact to yell over his shoulder at the officers to pursue it. He disappears inside the house with his gun still drawn.

Josh moves off me and starts to get up, but I clamp down on his arm.

"I think we should wait until Travis tells us to move."

He lifts his head and surveys the yard. "I think they're gone. You heard the truck."

"What if they weren't alone?"

He bites his lip. "I don't think we were the intended target, Autumn."

I check over my shoulder while letting Josh help me to my feet. I feel my muscles practically protest when I stand. I know I'm going to be stiff tomorrow. Turning thirty-four in June seemed like the turning point for my body. I have more aches and pains and I even found several gray hairs among my copper locks. Luckily, Regina covered them for me last week. Thoughts of Regina enter my mind. Did Regina just shoot up Eddie's house? I know she's involved in all of this, but how and why? She's not a criminal, right? A rule breaker, yes, but a killer, I just don't see it. There has to be more going on, but what? I brush off my clothes and glance over at Violet. Josh helped her up and now, she's clinging to him while he talks gently to her. Tears are falling down her face as she stares at the front door.

Travis still hasn't come out and neither has Eddie. I

know Travis told me to stay put, but what if Eddie is...I can't even wrap my mind it.

A siren sounds down the street and an ambulance comes into view.

Eddie.

My legs carry me across the driveway and to the front steps before I even realize what I'm doing. Josh catches my arm before I go inside.

"Autumn. Maybe we should wait outside." His blue eyes are dark and pleading.

I try to wrestle out of his grasp, but he holds tight.

Two male paramedics hurry past me with a stretcher and disappear inside. My heart is thumping loudly and I can barely catch my breath. Eddie can't die. We haven't solved his mother's case. She needs our help. He needs to see her. This can't be happening. Panic sets in and I feel my chest tightening. My throat feels like it's closing in and I gasp for air. Oh no, this is not the time for a panic attack, but I can't stop it. I grip Josh's arm.

It only takes him a second to realize what's happening. "Breathe, Autumn. Deep breaths. In through your nose and out through your mouth. Focus on your breath." He takes my hands. "You're freezing. How is that possible? It's muggy out here."

I ignore him because I have no idea why I'm so cold. My teeth begin to chatter as I gulp for air. My breathing is shallow. I try to take a deep breath, but it feels like a giant is squeezing my lungs with his huge hand and won't let go. I shut my eyes and sway slightly. I'm getting light headed.

"Autumn, listen to me. We're going to sit down on the sidewalk, ok."

My eyes flutter open as we flop down on the ground. The smooth stones on the sidewalk are cool despite the

August heat. I close my eyes and run my hand over them. Finally, I'm able to take a deep breath and the pressure on my lungs ceases.

"Are you alright?"

I hear the creak of the stretcher and snap my gaze up to the paramedics in front of me. My teeth are still chattering when I ask, "Is-Is he..." I can't say it. A tear falls from my eye and runs down my cheek.

The middle-aged blond paramedic, Rick shakes his head. "He's fine. Refused to go to the hospital though."

"He's fine?" I'm not sure I believe him.

He nods. "Just a few cuts from shattered glass and a deeper cut that really needs stitches, but he's refusing to get it looked at. Guess the guy hates hospitals." Rick shrugs. "And the sight of blood. He passed out. When Travis saw all the blood, he immediately called us." He studies me again. "You don't look so good. Why are you shivering?"

"She had a panic attack," Josh informs him.

He bends down and checks my pulse. "Your pulse is elevated. Do you feel like you're running a fever?"

"No."

"Why don't we go over to the ambulance and we'll check you out?"

I open my mouth to object when his radio goes off.

He responds to the operator and seems torn on what to do.

"I'm fine," I assure him.

He frowns like he doesn't believe me.

"Really. Go. Save lives." I force a smile.

He gets up hesitantly and makes me promise to go to the ER if I start feeling worse.

I promise him I will as he hurries down the driveway.

"I think you should go lie down, Autumn." Josh gets up and holds out a hand to help me to my feet.

Violet is hovering by the garage door. Her eyes are wide and her lower lip is quivering. "He's ok?"

At her words, the weight lifts off my chest and I can take another breath before standing up on shaky legs. I pat Josh's hand and motion to the front door. "Let's check on Eddie first."

"Autumn, you've had two incidents this morning. I think you need to go to the hospital and get checked out."

I shake my head because I know these "incidents" aren't me. They're Laura. I don't know how or why, but I know these are her feelings. I'm cold because she's cold. I felt her get shot and I felt her emotions when she thought something happened to Eddie. If I tell a doctor what's really going on, they'll lock me up and throw away the key.

"Autumn, you're as white as cotton. What's wrong?" Travis asks, stepping out of the house and walking toward me.

"She had a panic attack," Josh informs him.

"What? Why? Was it the shootings?" He rakes a hand through his shaggy red hair. "I knew I should have had the officers check the woods."

"It wasn't the shooting." Josh frowns and narrows his eyes at me. "She couldn't catch her breath when the ambulance showed up." He doesn't mention the spa, which I'm grateful for. I don't want to explain Laura to Travis. He doesn't believe in ghosts and anything paranormal freaks him out.

Travis studies me. "You were worried about Eddie?"

I take another deep breath. How am I going to explain this to the guys? They're looking at me like they did when I started dating James. Sheesh. I agree to go on one date and don't even get to go on it and suddenly, I can't worry about another male. The testosterone is rolling off them. I wonder why Travis even cares. He's dating Allison. I'm no longer his concern. Something I think I'll tell him. "Eddie is my friend. Of course, I was worried. You don't need to worry about me. I'm fine, but I'm sure Allison has heard about the shooting. You should probably call and let her know you're okay."

Travis cringes and his cheeks match his hair. He opens his mouth to say something when Eddie steps onto the front step. "It's not safe for you to be out in the open." Travis puts a hand to his gun and scans the yard before moving toward Eddie. "In fact, I think we all need to move indoors. It's not safe for any of us to be out here."

8

"We can go to my house," I offer.

Eddie gives me a relieved smile. His arms are bandaged and there's a square bandage on his left cheek.

"I need to stay and meet the forensic team. Mr. Bell, do you have somewhere to stay until we catch whoever is trying to..." His voice trails off. He doesn't need to finish his sentence. We all know Eddie has a target on his back.

I open my mouth to offer my guest room, but Josh pipes up, "He can stay with me."

Eddie and Travis both gape at him like he has a third eye. I smirk because I know why he's offering and it has nothing to do with being neighborly.

"Are you sure?" Eddie runs a hand over the back of his neck like he's unsure about Josh's offer.

"Of course." Josh shrugs like it's no big deal.

"Can I grab a few things?" Eddie turns to Travis.

"I'll escort you." Travis motions to the house. "Autumn, you, Violet and Josh need to get inside. I'll bring Eddie over when he's done. I also need to get your statements."

I nod and turn toward my house. Once we're out of earshot of Eddie, I ask, "Need any help getting the guest room ready?" I bump his arm with mine and he rolls his eyes at me.

"It's ready. You haven't slept over in a while so it's good to go."

"Mmmhmm."

"What? You haven't." He elbows me.

I snort. "It's so nice of you to offer your guest room to Eddie."

"Just being neighborly."

"Let's go to your house for lunch so Eddie can get settled in the guest room." I stop by the garage doors and take in a shell-shocked Violet. "Violet, want to go with us or wait for Eddie?"

She seems to snap out of her trance. The poor girl is beyond traumatized today. "I'll wait for Eddie."

"Let him know we went to Josh's house."

She nods and hurries inside.

We cross the bushes that divide our yards and start up his sidewalk. "What's on the menu?"

Josh unlocks his front door and turns on the lights. "Couch for you. I'll make enchiladas after I check to make sure there are clean towels for Eddie." He heads to the guest room while I ignore his order and head to the kitchen.

His ranch style house has the same open floor plan as mine. The front door opens into the living room with the kitchen and eat-in dining room off to the right. His master is behind the kitchen while an office, guest room, and bath are off the living room.

I rifle through the fridge and grab out some chicken and peppers for our guests. I'm relieved to see some kale and berries for me to make a smoothie too. I grab some almond butter and am pulling out the blender when Josh walks in.

He frowns. "I told you to rest."

"I'm fine. Probably just need to eat a little something." My stomach growls at the mention of food.

Josh takes over cooking the chicken and dicing veggies.

I busy myself with making smoothies. My thoughts drift back to my vision at the spa and then my "panic attack" at Eddie's. Laura and I are connected somehow, but why... how? I've been digging into her background and the only thing we've discovered is she opened the salon with Regina. They met in cosmetology school and Regina convinced her to move to Daysville and open up a salon with her. There's a newspaper article about her marrying Dean Smoot, but nothing on her death or murder. I asked Beverly the librarian about the missing archives, but she insisted everything was there. She's been scouring the papers for the past few weeks to prove me wrong. So far, she hasn't found them either. It seems someone doesn't want us to find out anything about Laura Smoot's death or the investigation. I think back to Laura's words. *I don't know where it is.* What was she referring to? Did she have something someone wanted? Something worth killing her for? What did you get yourself into, Laura?

"What was that?" Josh turns toward me with a spatula in his hand.

I blush. I must have been mumbling to myself. "Nothing."

He frowns again and focuses back on the enchilada sauce. "You're hiding something, Autumn."

I open my mouth to protest when there's a knock on the front door. "I'll get it." I snag to go cup for the smoothie.

Josh raises an eyebrow at me.

"It's for Travis. He probably hasn't had anything to eat today." I know I shouldn't care if he eats or not, but with Regina missing, I know he's focusing all his energy on finding her and not taking care of himself. Travis will always be my friend no matter what and friends take care of each other, right?

I open the door to find Eddie with a couple bags in his hands and Violet clinging to his bicep. Travis is looking over their shoulders. "Come in." I gesture for them to enter. I point Eddie down the hall so he can drop off his luggage. He thanks me and takes off in that direction while Violet moves to the kitchen.

When I turn back to Travis, I see him already making his way down the sidewalk. So, I guess now, we're not talking to each other. Great. "Travis." He keeps walking. "Travis." I hurry down the front steps and meet him on the driveway before he finally stops.

His shoulders are hunched forward and he seems annoyed.

"Thought you might want a smoothie." I hold out the to-go cup to him.

He eyes it and shakes his head. "No, thanks. I'm not hungry."

I blink and wonder if I heard him correctly. Travis is always hungry. "Really?"

His stomach growls in protest.

I stifle a grin. "Sounds like you are."

"I'll grab something on the way back to the station."

"Huh? Why? I have a smoothie right here for you and it's free."

He studies the food then looks me in the eye and says, "No, it's not." He spins on his heels and marches over to Eddie's house.

I'm speechless, which is rare for me. What does he mean this smoothie isn't free? Um, yes, it is. I look down at the cup and realize his comment had nothing to do with the smoothie. I fight the urge to race across the yard and interrogate him. I should go over there and demand he tell me what he knows about Regina. Also, why he failed to tell he's dating Allison. Not to mention, why he's avoiding me.

Several police cars pull up in front of Eddie's house and the forensic team is right behind them. Now, isn't the time to interrogate Detective Mills, but I will. I sigh and make my way back into the house. Josh and Eddie are eating chips and guacamole at the kitchen counter.

Josh's eyebrows shoot to his hairline when he sees me with the smoothie still in my hand. "Travis wasn't hungry?"

"Something like that," I mumble and take a sip of the smoothie.

"Thanks for letting me stay here, Josh." He pauses and fiddles with a tortilla chip then says, "I don't want to put you or Autumn in danger though."

Josh shakes his head. "Unlike Autumn, I put in a security system after April's murder and I bought a gun."

My jaw drops open. "Y-You have a gun?"

He stares into the guacamole, not meeting my eyes. "I want to be able to protect you if I need to... if Travis isn't around."

I kind of melt at his words, but I'm still in shock. We aren't gun people. I mean we have nothing against guns, but we aren't hunters and we never felt the need to have one in Daysville...until recently. "Why didn't you tell me?"

"I wanted to feel confident using it first."

I gulp thinking about my shy and peace-loving friend using a gun. It's so unlike him, but I can't blame him for everything we've been through the past few months. I reach out and place a hand over his. He looks up from the bowl and I smile. He gives me a lopsided grin and I know we're good. At least one guy in my life is solid. I can always count on Josh no matter what.

Eddie's phone buzzes. He pops the chip in his mouth before checking it. His hand starts to shake and his face loses all color.

"What's wrong?"

His hands are shaking so badly, he almost drops the phone as he hands it to me.

My eyes widen when I read the text. "Who sent this to you?"

"It's from a blocked number."

"Probably trying to scare you or get you to go outside."

"Should I?" He gets up quickly, knocking over the bar stool.

"What's going on?" Josh rights the stool then gestures to the phone.

I hold up the phone and his eyes go wide.

"Call Travis. I'll get my gun." He moves to his bedroom.

I want to call out to him to forget the gun, but bite my tongue. We may need it.

"What's going on?" Violet asks, coming out of the bathroom.

"Eddie got another threat. There's something in his trunk." I think back to the text. *Like my surprises so far? Check your trunk.* I shiver, pondering what could be in his trunk.

Her mouth drops open then she darts over to Eddie, who has started pacing in front of Josh's couch.

Josh comes out of the master bedroom with a pistol in his hand.

The sight of it makes me cringe. I really don't like guns.

"Violet, stay here. Don't leave the house for any reason."

He hands her the house phone; yes, Josh still has a landline for some unknown reason. "Call the police if you hear anything unusual. I'll set the alarm system so you'll be safe in here."

Violet nods and whispers to Eddie.

He pats her hand then moves over to us. A determined expression on his face.

Josh eyes me and sighs. "I'd tell you to stay put, but I know it's useless."

I smirk at him and roll my eyes. "Let me try Travis." I dial his number, but of course, he doesn't answer. This isn't the time to avoid me. I forward the text to him and meet Josh at the front door. My phone rings as we're making our way to Eddie's Mercedes.

Travis's deep voice asks, "Who sent you this?"

"If I knew, I would have included it in the text, but we're going to check it out now"

"We? No, you stay put, Autumn."

I hang up on him before he can talk me out of going. I glance over at Eddie's house. Travis's SUV is gone, but officers are still processing the scene.

Eddie's Mercedes is sitting in his driveway like a ticking time bomb...possibly a real one.

9

Sirens sound behind me and I wonder how many more times today I'll hear them. I mean it's only one and the whole morning has been packed with drama.

Travis leaps out of his SUV and runs over to us. "I told you to stay put. Why don't you ever listen, Autumn? There's someone out to get Eddie and you think having him out in the open checking out whatever's in his trunk is a smart idea? You could get him killed or hurt. Don't you ever think about anyone, but yourself?"

Tears blur my eyes and a lump forms in my throat.

Josh jumps to my defense. "Hey, that's uncalled for. Autumn's always thinking of others and she couldn't have stopped Eddie from coming out if she tried." He nods to Eddie for backup. "Right, man?"

Eddie narrows his eyes at Travis and says, "Autumn has been nothing but helpful and she didn't force me to come out here. If you think I'm going to sit around while someone threatens me, you're mistaken. There may be a clue to who's doing this in the trunk."

Travis runs a hand through his hair and mutters an apology, but it doesn't sound sincere. He moves to the trunk and holds out his hand to Eddie. "Where are your keys?"

Eddie drops them in his hands with a scowl on his face.

"We're going to duck behind my SUV then I'll open the trunk. One bomb scare today is enough."

We hurry to the SUV and duck behind it. Travis clicks the trunk.

I close my eyes and wait.

Nothing.

Travis peeks out from behind the SUV and glances around. He motions for a couple of officers to come over and flank us as we head back to the trunk. The officers have their guns drawn and their backs to us. It's like we have our own bodyguards.

We move slowly to the trunk.

Travis reaches it first. "What th-?" He puts a hand up to his nose to ward off the stench.

I peek over the edge and almost gag.

Travis turns to Eddie. "You didn't know this was back here?"

Eddie takes in the trunk. His throat bobs as he swallows and shakes his head.

Josh has his back turned. "I just ate. It smells awful. What is it?"

I pat his back. "It's a bunch of dead rats. Probably about twenty."

He cringes.

"Does someone think you're a rat, Mr. Bell?" Travis questions.

Eddie swallows again and runs a hand over the back of his neck, but doesn't say anything.

Travis turns to me. "Does this have anything to do with the 'investigating' you and Eddie are doing at the library?"

I shrug.

"Someone better start talking. I have a bomb planted at the church with a text message sent to Mr. Bell's phone, a break-in and shootout at Mr. Bell's home and now this." He gestures to the trunk. "What's going on?"

No one says anything.

"I can't protect you if I don't know what we're up against."

Eddie looks at me. I give him a closed-lipped smile and shrug again. This is his call. It's his mother's case.

"Let's go inside and I'll tell you everything."

Travis's eyes go wide for a moment like he's shocked we are going to let him in on our summer investigation then he motions for us to lead the way.

We all turn and head to the front door when a police car pulls up to the curb and a couple of officers get out. Travis stays back to talk to them for a few minutes before he joins us inside. When he shuts the front door, he looks flustered and unsure of what to do.

Josh is sitting in his recliner.

Violet and Eddie have taken the couch.

I'm in the plush loveseat.

Travis runs a hand through his hair and decides to sit on the fireplace.

I can't help but feel a little rejected by his seating choice. I try to remind myself he's dating Allison so it makes sense he wouldn't sit by me, right?

Travis clears his throat and looks at Eddie. "So, what's going on?"

Eddie glances at me and I nod. He seems unsure on whether or not to trust this group.

"I've already told Josh," I offer, hoping he won't be upset with me.

He cuts his gaze to Josh, who gives him a lopsided grin. Eddie sighs.

"She just told me this morning. I kind of forced her to tell me after the whole bomb incident," Josh says, knowing by the look on Eddie's face, he thinks I've betrayed his trust.

Eddie nods and gives me a sympathetic look. "I shouldn't have put you in that position, Autumn. I'm sorry."

Violet huffs next to him. "Why did you confide in Autumn when we're dating?"

Eddie's face turns red and he runs a hand over his jaw.

The room is silent while everyone waits for him to say something. The cuckoo clock ticks off the seconds on the wall behind us. When it seems he's not going to speak, I jump in to save him.

"Eddie heard about me solving the cases around town. He asked for my help in solving one that's very personal to him."

Violet doesn't appear satisfied with my explanation. "What's so personal you couldn't share it with your girlfriend?"

Eddie puts his head in his hands and whispers, "My mother's murder."

Violet gasps.

Travis's eyebrows raise, but otherwise, his face is stoic and unreadable.

Eddie sits up and takes a deep breath. "My real name is Walter Smoot."

Violet gasps again.

Travis clenches his jaw and fists for some reason.

"I would appreciate it if that didn't get out," he adds.

Everyone nods in agreement.

"I'm sure you all know the story about my mom's murder. The spa used to be a duplex. We lived there from the time I was born until she died when I was in kindergarten. I came home from the last day of school and found her in her bedroom. She'd been shot in the back."

I rub the spot on my chest. It burns a little. A chill fills the room. Laura. I wonder if Eddie can feel her.

He shivers slightly then continues, "My grandparents took me away and I lived with them in Villsboro for a few years before I came home from school one day to police cars in the driveway. A social worker told me they'd been murdered and I was going into foster care."

Violet puts an arm around him as tears fall down her cheeks.

I wipe away a couple of my own. This guy lost his whole family in such a short time and at such a young age. The room gets colder and I notice Josh looking over at the thermostat then at me. He tilts his head and I nod.

We both gaze over at Travis, who unrolls his long sleeves and rubs his hands together.

Violet snuggles into Eddie's side.

He puts his arm around her then continues, "A nice family adopted me. Changed my name to my middle name, Edward. Called me Eddie and I took their last name, Bell. My mother and grandparents' killer or killers were never found. The police didn't think the two crimes were related. Insisted both were just break-in's gone wrong, but I know they're related," he says, glancing at Josh, probably wondering why it's suddenly so cold in here.

Josh gets up and checks the thermostat. He's probably turning on the heat, which is crazy since it's the middle of August, but this room feels colder than a morgue.

Eddie continues, his teeth chattering slightly, "I went to

school in Chicago, got my law degree and worked for several big firms before I felt ready to come back here. Felt ready to face my past and solve my mother's murder...my grandparents' murders and bring their killer or killers to justice."

No one spoke. No one moved. We let Eddie's words sink in or maybe we're all frozen. I pull the fuzzy blanket off the back of the loveseat and wrap it around my shoulders.

Eddie rubs a hand up and down Violet's arm while she snuggles in closer. "When I came to town, I didn't know who I could trust then I kept hearing about the crime-solving massage therapist, Autumn Fisher." He grins at me.

I blush and tuck a strand of loose hair behind my ear.

Travis rolls his eyes.

"I remembered Autumn from kindergarten. She always stood up for me when Caleb Gallahan would pick on me."

Josh mutter something about Caleb Gallahan being the worst while he hands Violet a blanket. "Sorry guys the thermostat must be broken. I texted Shane to come over and look at it." He switches on the fireplace for Travis then winks at me before sitting back down in his chair.

Eddie wraps the blanket around Violet then continues, "When I met Autumn again after Mrs. Walls funeral, she remembered me and offered to help solve my mother's murder. That's what we've been doing at the library. Scouring newspaper archives and researching everything we can on the cases."

"And what did you find?" Travis asks, his eyes narrowed and suspicious. Why? Your guess is as good as mine.

"Only a few articles about her opening the salon with your aunt and marrying my dad, but nothing on her murder."

"She opened the salon with Regina?"

Eddie nods. "I didn't remember that. I knew she did hair,

but I rarely went to the shop. I always had a sitter on Saturdays and she never worked late during the week."

"How is there nothing on her murder? That's impossible. Daysville reports everything. There's no way they wouldn't report on your mother's murder." Travis gets up and begins to pace the room. His woodsy scent wafts through the air with every turn. I'm pretty sure he's pacing not because he's upset, but more so to get the blood flowing to his extremities. The temperature in this room has got to be in the thirties.

Eddie flexes his jaw. "It's not impossible. Autumn and I have gone through every archive, newspaper, and history book on Daysville. I've even gone through the reports from that time period and stuff is missing. There's nothing from the month she died or even six months prior to her death."

Travis stops pacing and gapes at Eddie then looks to me.

I nod. "Eddie's even having trouble securing the police reports on his mother's death and he's trying to get the reports on his grandparents too with little results."

Travis frowns. "You think someone in Daysville is behind your mother's murder? Behind your grandparents' murders?"

"Yes."

"Someone with enough power to make it difficult for Eddie to secure his family's files. They know who Eddie is and are trying their hardest to get rid of him. It has to be someone who has a lot to lose if Eddie figures out who killed his family."

Travis narrows his eyes at me. "Someone who probably knows you're helping him too."

I shrug, which only makes his jaw work overtime. I'm surprised he doesn't have TMJ with all the clenching he does.

"I'll make a few calls. Excuse me," Travis says then strides out the door.

Josh gets up as soon as he leaves and opens the windows and back door to the deck to try and warm up the room. "The enchiladas are almost done. They should help warm us up."

Violet and Eddie nod.

I get up and motion with my head to Josh that I'm going out front.

He smirks then turns to pull out the food from the oven.

I open the door to find a ranting and raving Travis on the phone. I quickly step out on the porch and shut the door behind me so Eddie can't hear him.

"What do you mean those files can't be found? Where are they?" He pauses then hangs up.

"You can't get them either?" I step up next to him.

He's clutching his phone so tightly in his hand, I wouldn't be surprised if it doesn't crack under his grip. "The files are gone. There's nothing in the evidence boxes. Nothing." He runs a hand through his hair.

"What about Eddie's dad?"

Travis raises an eyebrow. "Eddie's dad is dead, Autumn."

10

"How did you know that?"

"Doesn't matter. Why are you bringing him up?"

I eye him but decide to hold my questions until later. "He died in a car crash. What if the crash wasn't an accident? What if it was murder? What if his mom found out and threatened to expose the killer. Told her parents about it, which in turn got them killed." I take a breath in through my nose and out through my mouth because I'm rambling. The smell of fresh cut grass tickles my nose and makes me sneeze.

"Bless you," Travis says, glancing over his shoulder at Mr. Carlton, who is cutting his front lawn. "Let's go back inside before your allergies kick in."

Officer Roberts calls out to Travis and hurries up the sidewalk carrying an evidence bag with a piece of paper in it. "We found this among the rats." He hands it to Travis then smiles at me and pretends to tip his non-existent hat. He's in his late fifties with gray hair, rosy cheeks, and a protruding belly because he loves his wife's southern cooking. "Hey, Miss Autumn. How are you?"

I smile back at him. "I'm good, Fred. How's Margaret?"

He grins even wider. "She's really good. Making me meatloaf and mashed potatoes and gravy for dinner." His stomach growls at the mention of his impending meal. He chuckles then turns back to Travis, who hasn't said anything.

I peek over his shoulder and look at the piece of paper. The note makes me gasp. *Don't be a rat like your mom or you'll die like she did.*

"Have we been able to remove the rats from Mr. Bell's trunk?"

Officer Roberts nods. "The coroner just left with them although they were shot in the back so I'm not sure we really need to autopsy them."

"Make sure the coroner evaluates each one for human particulates. Any hair, fiber, skin cells, anything I want to know about it. Report directly to me. Got it, Fred."

Officer Roberts eyes grow wide and he steps back from Travis.

I glance at Travis. His face is red, his fists are clenched at his sides and the vein in his forehead has popped out and appears to have its own heartbeat. He's very intimidating and I can see why Fred is keeping his distance. I place a hand on Travis's arm and smile at Fred. "Eddie is really upset about this so Travis has promised to keep him informed about every detail."

Fred nods and hurries back down the driveway.

Travis rips his arm from my grasp. "Don't ever do that again," he snaps.

"What?"

"Undermine me in front of my officers."

"I wasn't...I didn't mean to. Fred just looked about ready to wet himself."

"This case is sensitive. I need them to realize that and report only to me. If someone higher up is behind this, evidence could go missing and we'll never solve this case." He runs a hand through his hair then meets my eyes. "And Eddie could end up dead or worse...you could."

I smile at him and reach out for his hand, but quickly pull it back. "Thank you for looking out for Eddie and for me. You're a great detective and a good friend."

He cringes at the word 'friend' but quickly recovers. "I'm glad you two finally told me what you've been up to. We can all work together to solve this now. You should have just told me to begin with and maybe we could have avoided today's incidents." He pauses then asks, "Do you not trust me, Autumn?"

I open my mouth to respond when Josh pokes his head out the front door.

"Eddie got another text. I think you should see it."

We rush inside.

The scent of baked chicken mixed with tomato sauce and spices greets us.

Travis's stomach growls next to me.

I smirk, knowing he never grabbed anything to eat. He should have taken me up on that "free" smoothie.

Eddie's standing at the kitchen counter with his palms on either side of the phone in front of him.

Violet is talking to him softly and rubbing his back.

"What's going on?" Travis asks, stepping up beside Eddie.

Eddie pushes the phone over to him.

Travis picks it up and stares at the screen. He drops the phone and I catch it before it clatters to the floor.

"What is it?" I turn the phone over and check out the screen. A picture of a smiling man and Laura holding Eddie or at that time Walter, fills the frame, but the person in the background catches my attention. I'd recognize that red hair anywhere. Regina. Only she wasn't smiling. She's glaring at the happy couple. "Travis, did Regina know Laura? Eddie found a picture of them together from Cosmetology school. It appears they went to the same school."

"Someone is trying to frame Regina," Travis growls. "They're watching. They know I'm here. That I'm talking to Eddie. They're threatening me by sending me this picture."

"You got all that from this picture?" I place the phone back on the counter.

Travis nods. "If I dig into this, they'll pin these murders on Regina. That's what that strange text meant the day she disappeared. *If I go down, you do too.* Someone is threatening her." Travis sighs. "I have to remove myself from this case."

"What?!" I screech.

He gives me a sympathetic look. "I'm sorry, Autumn. I can't let my aunt go to jail over something she didn't do."

I narrow my eyes at him. "Are you sure she's not involved somehow?"

He narrows his eyes right back at me. "You better watch what you're saying, Autumn. I know you're disappointed, but don't start pointing fingers at my aunt. The woman raised me and she's been like a second mother to you. How could you even accuse her of something so awful?"

I push back the guilt threatening to bubble to the surface. "Regina knew Eddie's mother and I'm assuming this man in the photo is your father, right, Eddie?"

Eddie nods although he's still bracing himself on the island. The air around him is ice cold and I can see his breath as he inhales and exhales.

I point at the phone, which is now black. "Regina is glaring at Eddie's parents. Why?"

Travis shrugs. "Maybe she was glaring at the person taking the photo."

I didn't think of that, but the fact Regina knew Eddie's parents is something to investigate. "You can't just quit, Travis. We need you. Your resources. Your expertise. We literally have nothing except for Regina being involved or a pawn and Eddie's mother being a rat." The words are out of my mouth before I can stop them.

Eddie whips around and glares at me. "What did you just say?"

Travis groans and glares at me before pulling the evidence bag from his pocket. "This was in with the rats." He hands it to Eddie, who takes it and studies the text.

"So, my mother was killed because she found out something she wasn't supposed to and was going to expose someone. Someone with a lot of power in this town. Who?"

Travis holds up his hands. "I'm out. I can't be involved. People are watching." He snatches the evidence bag from Eddie. "I'll keep you posted on the bomb, break-in, and the rats, but I won't dig any further. I can't risk it. I can't put Regina in any more danger. I hope you can understand." He pats Eddie on the back, who nods and thanks him for his time.

I, on the other hand, am ready to call Travis a bunch of names like coward and chicken, well I guess just two names, but I will flap my arms like a chicken for good measure. Before I can open my mouth, Travis is saved by his cell phone ringing.

"Are you sure?" He pauses and his face goes pale. "Ok, I'll be right there." He hangs up and runs out the door without a word.

11

I yawn and stretch. My back and neck go into a mini spasm from sleeping on Josh's couch. I glance at the cuckoo clock on the wall. It's just after seven and it's Monday. Sunday seemed to drag on and now, it's back to work.

Violet is sleeping opposite of me with her legs pinning me down. Great. I shift and lift her legs before slipping out from underneath her. Josh is asleep in the recliner and Eddie is draped over the loveseat. He's got to be uncomfortable.

I rub my eyes and make my way to the kitchen thinking about yesterday. We spent the afternoon eating enchiladas and making a suspect list. My stomach growls at the thought of food. Josh's vegan enchiladas were incredible and everyone else seemed to enjoy the chicken ones too.

The suspect list is on the counter next to my cell phone. I check to see if there's a text or call from Travis. Nothing. The rumor mill is strangely silent so I'm not sure if something actually happened or Travis was just trying to get out of here without me giving him a guilt trip. I'm voting for the latter.

I glance over at the suspect list. We spent hours debating motives and who in Daysville had enough power to make everything go away. By everything, I mean case files, evidence boxes, archives, newspapers and who knows what else. This person or persons must have either threatened or paid people off to cover up and/or destroy things.

The old mayor was at the top of the list, but I'm not sure he has much influence in town anymore. He's pretty much holed himself up in his mansion on the hill and rarely shows his face around town. Charges are still pending against him from stealing money from the city.

Next up, there's the police captain Paul Rivers. The captain's married, but supposedly he and Regina used to date. He's at the top of my list and it's not just because I don't like him. The captain has been known to cut corners and make things disappear for the "good of the town." He's a shady guy and doesn't deserve his title. I'm counting down the days till he retires. Hopefully, Travis will step into his shoes. He'd make a great captain and he'd be off the streets, which means he'd be out of harm's way. One of the reasons I'm hesitant to move forward with him...what if I lost him? I can't let him in again, love him again and then lose him. The thought guts me. I push it down and focus on the next suspect.

Judge Charles Holliday. He's Harold's twin brother. He lost his wife to an aneurysm a few years back and has never remarried. He could have retired last year, but he loves what he does and wants to continue his duty until he no longer can. He's a stickler for the rules and is the best judge Daysville has ever had. He also has a lot of power in this town. The whole Holliday family does. Their family has been in Daysville since the beginning and has sunk a ton of time and money into making Daysville what it is today. Well, what it was before all these murders started.

The next name on the list and after lots of arguing is Harold Holliday from Harold's Hardware. Josh is upset we even have him on the list. He loves Harold. We all do, but he's a respected member of the community and he's super paranoid. Everyone says it's PTSD from the war, but from what I found out in doing my research this summer, Harold never went to war and he never served in the military. I was shocked, to say the least, and when I told Josh he wanted proof. I showed him the pictures I found on Harold Holliday, which show him in the background leaving Daysville, not with the other men heading off to serve, but in a psychiatric van. The image was small and most people would probably miss it, but I was able to blow it up and there's no mistaken Harold in a strait jacket with a wild look in his eye. After a little more digging, I found out Harold suffered a mental break down shortly after graduating high school. His parents told everyone he went away to war, but he really went off to a mental institution. Unfortunately, no other men came back from war so no one could contradict their story.

Harold came back to Daysville a few months before Eddie's father died. Could he have killed Eddie's family because they found out his secret or did someone in his family kill them to keep his secret safe? I sigh and my heart aches at the thought of sweet Harold doing something so awful or feeling like he has to lie about his mental health. It's nothing to be ashamed of. Why did his family hide it from everyone?

Several other names were written then crossed out. The last one on the list is Harold and Harry's younger brother, Dave. He owns the Dollar and Dime shop in Daysville. While he doesn't have a ton of power in Daysville, he's still a Holliday. Eddie also found a picture of him with his father. They were apparently best friends as they were pictured together quite often in the newspaper. Town picnics, holiday parties and other social gatherings. These men were always talking or hanging out with Laura and Eddie's father, Dean.

"Anyone else we should add?"

I jump and knock the paper onto the floor.

Eddie bends down and picks it up. He's still in his suit from yesterday, which is beyond wrinkled. We're all still in our church clothes. Too focused on the case to bother to change. Time is not on our side and we have to figure this out before Eddie gets hurt or worse. "Sorry, didn't mean to scare you. I better jump in the shower and head into the office. I have several cases going in front of Judge Holliday today."

"Do you think he killed your family or knows who did?"

Eddie's brown eyes grow dark. "I hope not. I really like the guy. He's a great judge and you don't find that very often. I'd hate to lose him or find out he's crooked." He turns and heads toward the guest bathroom then stops just at the end of living room. "Thanks for this, Autumn. I couldn't do it without you."

I smile as he heads back to the guest room.

Josh clears his throat and gets out of the chair. "You sure nothing's going on between you two?" he whispers so Violet doesn't hear.

"Positive," I say a little loudly in case Violet is eavesdropping. "I better head home and grab a shower. We actually have a semi-busy day at the spa today." I'm a little giddy about it. Why? Well, today I have all reflexology clients.

Reflexology is my favorite modality. Josh thinks I have a foot fetish, but I'm almost ninety eight percent sure I don't. I mean have you ever had your feet rubbed? It's incredible, right? Sigh. I turn back to Josh. "Meet you at eight to head over to the spa?"

He nods and moves toward the master bedroom.

I open the front door and step out into the humid August morning. The sky is overcast so maybe we'll get some rain today. We definitely need it. The grass looks like straw planted in the ground and the poor plants are drooping. I bet if they could, they would be panting right now.

As I make my way across Josh's yard, I glance over at Eddie's house. A light is on in the front window. Huh? I wonder if Eddie forgot to turn it off. The curtains move and I freeze. Maybe it's just my imagination. I stare at the window a little longer, but don't see anything. My eyes must be playing tricks on me. Good thing I have my eye doctor appointment tomorrow.

I start moving toward my house again. When I reach the bushes, I catch a faint scent of smoke. I sniff the air again just to be sure. It's too early for someone to be burning brush not to mention the town has a no burn advisory posted until further notice. I sniff the air again and it's definitely smoke.

I look up and down the street to see where it's coming from when I hear the faint sound of a smoke alarm going off. I take off toward my house. *Please don't let it be on fire.* I've had enough home repairs lately. Caleb's body on my kitchen floor comes to mind and I push it away. Now, is not the time to rehash what happened in the spring.

My palms are sweaty, making my keys slippery and I drop them twice then pause to listen. The beeping is kind of muffled. If the smoke was in my house, it would be blaring right now. I glance over at Josh's house. It's quiet. No one's running out and gagging from smoke inhalation. My heart speeds up and a sinking feeling settles in the pit of my stomach.

Eddie's house.

I dial the fire station just as Eddie's front window explodes. Flames shoot out like there's a fire breathing dragon inside his house. A firetruck with lights on, but no siren is barreling down the street before the operator even picks up. I hang up. That's strange. How did they know Eddie's house was on fire? Maybe I should add the fire chief, Bob Billings, to the suspect list. Before I can dive into my theory on Chief Billings, another front window bursts into flames.

"Autumn! My house!" Eddie rushes over to me. His dark suit and white shirt are pressed, but his striped tie is hanging loosely around his neck. "What happened?"

I start to tell him about seeing someone in his house when Chief Billings comes rushing over to us. What is he doing at the fire? He never comes out on calls anymore. Maybe he was already here.

Chief Billings' black boots hit the pavement with a thud as he stops in front of us. His starched white shirt is tucked in, revealing his bulging belly, which is hanging over his belt and his black pants are plastered to his thighs. He wipes a hand over his bald head in an attempt to get rid of a bunch of sweat pouring down his face. He sure is sweating a lot considering the sun isn't even out. "Morning. The guys should have this out in no time. Anybody or any pets still inside?"

Eddie shakes his head.

"Good." He brushes off more sweat from his forehead. "It really went up quick. You'll want to call your insurance company right away. My guess is it's a total loss. Those flames were everywhere when we got here."

"How did you get here so fast, Chief? I was just dialing the station when the front window blew out."

Eddie cringes at my words.

He furrows his brow and cocks his head to the side. "Someone called it in."

"Really? Who?"

He shrugs. "Marge took the call." He studies me for a moment then says, "We'll know the cause of the fire later today. It's probably electrical."

Eddie frowns. "I just bought the house. Had it inspected. The inspector said everything was good."

Chief Billings shakes his head. "Mice or rats can chew through the wires. It's just a matter of time before the exposed wire short circuits causing a spark or heats up enough to catch debris on fire."

No one says anything for a moment while we take in the scene. A couple firefighters are aiming the hose at the flames while another one hovers by the fire hydrant.

"Well, I better check on my crew. I'll call you when I know more." Chief Billings nods his head and takes off toward the fire truck.

"Rats?" Eddie turns to me.

"Interesting rodent choice. Although, not uncommon."

"Should we add the Fire Chief to our suspect list?"

"I think so."

"Eddie, what's going on?" Violet rushes up to us. Her face is flushed, her hair is sticking up in the back and her dress is rumpled.

"Fire." He gestures to the house as if she can't see it for herself. The flames are dying down, but smoke is still billowing from the open door and windows.

"Oh no!" She covers her mouth with her hands. "How bad is it?"

Eddie shrugs.

"I'm sure it's not bad," she offers as a shutter falls off the house.

Josh comes up behind me and whispers, "Someone started this, didn't they?"

I gasp and remember the curtain moving. I almost forgot about it. "Eddie, I saw something."

He turns to me with a raised eyebrow. "What do you mean?"

"I mean I saw a light on in your front window and the curtains moving as I was walking home."

"So, rats didn't start the fire?"

"I don't know." I bite my lip, questioning my eyesight. Having my eyes checked can't come soon enough. "Did you leave a light on?"

He shakes his head. "Everything's been off since yesterday. I even double checked after dinner and set the alarm." He pauses. "Did you hear an alarm going off?"

"Just the smoke detectors."

"Huh? I'm sure I set the alarm." He frowns. "Maybe I forgot."

A crash inside the house draws our attention.

Eddie groans. "It's a total loss, isn't it?"

Violet pats his shoulder.

Another crash makes Eddie cringe.

Sirens sound down the street and we all turn in that direction. Travis's SUV comes barreling down the street and skids to a stop in front of us. He jumps out while another police car comes to a stop next to his. Travis rushes up to Eddie and jerks his arms behind his back, slapping on a pair of handcuffs. "You're under arrest for the murder of Regina Mills."

12

I pace the waiting area of the police station, my shoes squeaking with each pass. The officer behind the counter keeps shooting me annoyed looks, but I don't care. Maybe he'll call Travis to finally come out here and talk to me.

I've been at the police station all day and it's almost five o'clock. Well, not all day; I did go to the spa and see my reflexology clients. Only because Eddie insisted I go, but as soon as I was finished, I hightailed it over here. Josh stayed behind to take walk-ins and keep an eye on Maggie. She's been a little off lately. Kind of spacey and really jumpy every time the bell rings above the spa door. It's like she's expecting someone, but then looks relieved when it's only a client. She had a full afternoon of appointments so Josh agreed to close up. I'll have to figure out what's going on with her later. Right now, my focus is on Eddie and how to get him out of this mess.

Eddie killing Regina. I can't even wrap my mind around it. My stomach even turns at the thought. There's no way she's dead. She's too stubborn to die. If I were a betting woman, I'm not, but if I were, I would say Regina will outlive all of us. I shake my head and think about yesterday. Eddie was with us practically the whole day. There's also no possible way he killed her. Eddie's not a killer. Plus, he has no motive.

My phone buzzes in my pocket, but I ignore it. Everyone in town has been blowing up my phone. No one can believe our PA killed Regina. I've been trying to get them to quit jumping to conclusions without any proof, but no one's listening. They're holding a candlelight vigil in the parking lot of the salon at seven so hopefully, I'll know more by then and can set the record straight.

My phone buzzes again. I sigh and check it. Cat. She keeps texting me, asking me if the rumors are true about her aunt being dead because her father won't give her a straight answer. I quickly send her the same response I have all day. *No one knows anything. I'll text when I do. Try not to worry.* I know it's useless. The poor girl's a mess. Regina has been an aunt/grandma to her since she was born.

I sigh and tuck my phone back into my black scrub pocket then glance over at the seat by the window. Violet is chewing her nails although I don't think she has any left. She's been here since they arrested Eddie. They haven't told her anything or even let her see Eddie. The poor girl's a wreck. I tried to get her to go home to shower and change, but she won't. So, we've been camped out together in the waiting room for the past three hours.

The coroner walks out and stops at the front desk. I stop pacing and slide over to the front door. Since Travis is refusing to see me or talk to me, I'll get my information elsewhere.

From who?

Greg Pillman.

The coroner.

Greg and I went to high school together. He was valedictorian. We were always lab partners in school. He's super smart and we both share an appreciation for the human body. My appreciation is more in terms of helping alleviate pain in living humans while Greg's is more in terms of finding out the cause of death. His job is much harder, but someone has to do it.

I fidget by the door. He keeps droning on about the Luke Bryan concert Friday night. I almost forgot about it. I'll have to text Nikki and cancel. There's no way I can go with everything going on. She's going to be livid, but Eddie needs my help and there's not a moment to spare. Finally, Greg stops talking and I practically bound over to him like Tigger in *Winnie the Pooh*. "Hi, Greg."

"Autumn, hey. How are you?" He pushes his thick black glasses up his thin nose. They're really too big for his hollow blue eyes and sunken cheeks. I feel like I should offer to take him out for a cheeseburger and a large pizza. He looks about ready to blow away and his dark blue scrubs are practically hanging off him.

"I'm good. You?" I bat my eyelashes and give him a big smile. Tone it down, Autumn. Play it cool. My palms begin to sweat so I stick my hands in my scrub pockets.

He swipes a hand over his crew cut blond hair. His hair is so light it almost looks like he's bald. "Pretty good. It's been a busy day. I'm sure you've heard."

I nod. "Is it true?"

He glances around, takes my arm and pulls me over to the door. "I'm not at liberty to discuss open cases with the general public."

"I'm not the general public, Greg. I'm Autumn. Your

friend." I pat his shoulder and give him another grin. "Remember in biology, I let you dissect my frog."

He shakes his head and fights a smile. "Only because you were about to throw up on me."

I make a face, remembering the formaldehyde smell. My stomach turns and I fight the urge to gag. I knew I shouldn't have eaten that "fruit" from the vending machine. It did not look like mandarin oranges. I've got to start carrying a protein bar in my bag. I push down my gag reflex and focus on Greg. "It wasn't that bad. I just knew how much you liked to dissect things so I let you."

Greg blushes. "Alright, but you didn't hear this from me and it doesn't leave this room."

I nod. My heart starts to race and my palms go damp with sweat. The thought of hearing Regina's dead will probably be too much for me, but I have to know. I need to know. Right now. I gulp and steel myself for the news.

"Regina's car was found on the outside of town." He glances around and leans toward me. "It was empty."

"I thought..."

Greg puts a finger to my lips. "Let me finish."

I nod again and keep my mouth shut.

"The car was empty, but it was covered in blood. Regina's blood and Eddie's fingerprints were on the steering wheel."

I don't say anything while I wait for him to continue.

"There's no body. Every officer in town is searching for her, but no one has found her yet...well, her body."

When it looks like he's not going to say anything else, I ask, "Are you sure she's dead?" My voice comes out breathy and a little raspy. Emotion bubbles up to the surface and I blink back tears.

"The amount of blood in the car leads me to think so. It

was a lot of blood, Autumn." He takes my hand and gives it a squeeze. "I'm sorry. I know you two were close."

I wipe away a tear with my free hand while my brain absorbs this information. "How can Eddie's fingerprints be in her car? He was with us all day yesterday."

"All day?"

I pause. "Well, not all day, but still he didn't even know Regina. Why would he kill her?"

"You haven't heard?"

I furrow my brow. "Heard what?"

"Regina killed his parents and his grandparents."

My jaw drops. "What?"

Greg nods. "There was a tape of her admitting to the crimes in the glovebox. Eddie made her confess before he… well before he lost it and killed her."

I sway slightly.

Greg catches my arm. "Autumn, are you alright?"

I shake my head. "I need to sit down."

Greg ushers me over to a chair then hurries to grab me some water. "Here." He shoves the cup of water into my hand. "Drink this."

I guzzle down the water. It feels like I have cotton balls stuffed in my throat and the water is doing nothing to get rid of it. I put my head between my knees while Greg rubs my back with one hand and checks my pulse with another.

"I think she's in shock," Greg says to someone.

A shadow bends down in front of me. "Autumn?"

I lift my head and see the familiar green eyes I used to love to look into. Let's be honest, I still love to look into them, even though Travis is dating someone else. "Is it true?"

Travis furrows his brow. "Is what true?"

"Is Regina…" I can't even say it. Tears brim my eyes and the lump in my throat is feeling like I swallowed a softball.

He shoots a glare at Greg, who cringes.

Oops, I wasn't supposed to say anything. Shoot. Way to go, Autumn. Now, you've lost your ally in the police department.

"We aren't at liberty to discuss the case with civilians." He emphasizes civilians, probably to prove a point to Greg.

"I forgot, I have a meeting." Greg pops up from his seat then sends me a small smile before leaving. "Feel better, Autumn."

I smile back, relieved he doesn't seem upset with me.

"Can you stand?" Travis holds out a hand to me.

I nod and try to get to my feet. My knees buckle and I collapse into Travis's arms. He holds me tight and practically drags me back to his office. His woodsy cologne is usually intoxicating and soothing, but today, it makes me sad. Regina bought him his first bottle of cologne our freshman year of middle school after some of the boys teased him about being smelly after football practice. I got him the same cologne every year on his birthday after that…until we broke up.

He pulls me into his office and shuts the door firmly behind us.

I plop down into the chair across from his desk and try to push back nausea simmering in my belly.

Travis sits down in his desk hair and places both arms on his desk, clasping his hands together. "This whole case isn't what you think it is, Autumn."

I perk up at his words. "So, Regina's not dead?"

His face turns white before he shakes his head. "I'm not sure. I hope not, but the evidence doesn't look promising."

"Oh," I say, dread filling me again.

"Eddie Bell doesn't exist."

I quirk an eyebrow at him. "What are you talking about? Of course, he exists."

Travis runs a hand over his face. "No, he doesn't. Neither does Walter Smoot."

"Travis, you're not making any sense."

He sighs. "Walter Smoot died when he was seven years old. He was shot and killed along with his grandparents." He pauses to let the words sink in. "There was never an adoption. No one changed his name. Whoever that man in is in the interrogation room, it isn't Walter Smoot."

My mouth goes dry. I can't believe what I'm hearing. Why didn't I check out his story? Why do I just fall for things without doing the research? I was just so eager to help Laura. Laura. "I have to go." I jump up from my seat, scooting the chair across the tile floor.

"What? Where?" Travis stands, giving me a "you're crazy" kind of look.

"I forgot...the vigil for Regina is tonight."

Travis glances at his watch. "It's only five-thirty. That's not until seven."

I break out in a sweat. I'm so bad at lying, especially to Travis. "I-I need to change and eat."

"Autumn, I know this is a shock. Don't you want to talk about it?"

Before I can say anything, there's a knock on Travis's door. Allison pokes her pretty red head inside and my nausea kicks back in.

"Oh, sorry. Am I interrupting something?"

Her sweet southern drawl grates on my nerves. Has she always sounded like a Southern belle?

Travis opens his mouth, but I cut him off. "Of course not,

Travis was just giving me some instructions for tonight's vigil for Regina."

He purses his lips but doesn't rebut my fib.

Allison shifts uncomfortably on her three-inch red heels. They match her ruby red lips. Her long dark red hair hangs in loose waves that almost touch her curvy hips. She's wearing a tight black dress that only accentuates her curves. Ugh. She's like the poster girl for fitness.

I send her a closed-lipped smile and don't even bother looking at Travis before leaving his office in a rush. My heart's beating fast and tears are filling my eyes causing me to collide with someone in front of me. No arms go out to steady me so I almost face plant in the hall.

"Autumn, are you alright?"

I look up into what I thought were familiar dark eyes. "You lied to me," I spat. My voice is filled with venom and I almost don't recognize it.

Eddie or whoever he is has his hands cuffed behind his back. His suit is wrinkled and his hair is sticking up in different directions like he's been running his hands through it. "Whatever Travis told you is a lie. I didn't die. I'm Walter Smoot. I've never lied to you, Autumn." His face is red and his eyes are pleading with me to understand. "Someone is trying to discredit me. They've erased my whole life. Please, you have to believe me. I didn't do any of this. You know me."

I study him. He seems genuine, but he may just be a really good liar.

"Let's go," Fred nods to me before gently nudging Eddie towards the holding cells.

I watch him go. He turns and shoots me a look between pleading and defeated. Maybe he's not lying. My stomach starts to churn again as I make my way to the exit.

Violet pops up and rushes over to me as soon as the door opens. "It's not true. Eddie is who he says he is. I can prove it."

"How?" I cross my arms across my chest. I feel like I'm being torn in a million directions.

"Eddie or Walter fell when he was in kindergarten, remember?"

I rack my brain, trying to think back that far. "Vaguely. So?"

"Remember, we were playing sharks and minnows and he decided to climb the tree by the playground to get away from Josh."

The memory starts to come back to me.

"He fell, broke his arm and sliced his thigh on one of the branches. Bark even stuck in the wound. Blood was everywhere."

This wasn't doing anything to get rid of my nausea. "I remember," I mumble.

"He got stitches in his leg and there's a scar. I saw it when he was wearing shorts one day. We talked about it. He knew everything about that day. There's no way he's anyone else. I mean he knew details no one else could have known."

I'm more confused than ever. How could Travis tell me Eddie didn't exist and Walter is dead? If that's not Eddie in there, then who is it? And why would they be trying to solve Laura's murder if they weren't her son? The whole thing doesn't make sense. Did someone erase Eddie's life? Pay someone to feed the police false information? I need to get to a computer and then the spa.

I open my mouth to tell Violet I have to go when a commotion behind me draws my attention and then a popping sound fills the air.

13

"Autumn, you should go home," Travis hands me a cup of chamomile tea. Where he got chamomile tea in the hospital, I have no clue.

Yes, I'm in the hospital.

Why?

Well, that popping sound was a gun. Fred and the captain were interrogating Eddie or whoever he is, and according to Fred, Eddie went for Fred's gun and the captain shot him. He's been in surgery for…I glance up at the clock on the wall in the waiting room.

Three hours.

How can surgery take three hours? Something about the bullet being lodged in his lungs and I guess he's crashed a couple times. I know Dr. Gregory is taking good care of him, yet I can't help but worry.

Captain Rivers strides into the waiting room and scans it before his eyes fall on me then shift over to Travis. "Detective Mills, a moment."

Travis squeezes my knee before heading over to his boss.

I take a sip of tea and peer at the captain over the lip of

my cup. He's in good shape for pushing sixty. Besides his graying hair, you wouldn't guess him to be that old. He doesn't even have a bulging belly, just mounds of muscle, which push at the fabric of his white button-down shirt and black pants. His six-foot-three frame hovers over Travis, who is not short by any means, but he's still several inches shorter than the captain.

The captain keeps glancing over at me while he whispers with Travis. A chill runs down my spine and suddenly, the room is ice cold.

Laura.

I rub my arms. Everyone else in the waiting room gets up and moves outside to warm up. Outside, even at almost nine o'clock at night is still in the upper seventies. Inside, the hospital feels like a freezer.

I reach for my phone to text Josh to bring me a sweatshirt. He went to Regina's vigil at my insistence. Someone needed to be there from our camp to show our support. I've been getting the cold shoulder from several locals at the hospital and numerous texts calling me a traitor and demanding to know why I've been helping a murderer.

I sigh, reading another mean text, then type out a quick text to Josh. If Eddie is really Walter then I think Laura will be staying put until she knows he's okay. I glance up to catch a shimmer of her hovering by Travis. Her face is pinched and her eyes are angry as she glares at the captain. Laura spots me, shakes her head then vanishes.

Shoot. I really need to talk to her. Well, maybe talk to her. The only thing she's done so far is point to the wall in the spa.

What is it with the wall? Was she indicating Regina killed her? Why? Why would Regina kill Dean, Eddie's father, then Laura, followed by her parents? It doesn't make any sense. I think back to the photo Eddie showed me. Regina was glaring at his parents. Why? If she killed them out of revenge, what did they do to her? I have to dig deeper.

Travis jolts me from my thoughts when he sits down next to me.

"Everything ok?"

He runs a hand over his face then puts his head in his hands. "They don't think he's going to make it."

I close my eyes and try to keep the tears at bay. This can't be happening.

Screams and shouts come from outside the door.

Travis and I exchange a look and hurry toward the noise.

The EMT, Rick bursts through the door with a stretcher. "Everyone move," he yells as he rushes past us.

I glance down at the stretcher and gasp. "Harold."

The wiry old man is ash gray, eyes closed and unmoving. There's no blood that I can see, but he's covered up to his neck.

Josh runs in behind them and practically barrels me over.

"Whoa." I grab his arm to steady us both "What's going on?"

"Harold," He gasps for air and puts his hands on his knees. "He-He" Josh gulps for more air.

"Sit down," I gesture to the chair behind us.

He slides into it and takes a few more breaths.

"I was leaving the vigil and saw a light on in the hardware store. Harold never leaves the lights on so I went to check it out. The front door was open a crack so I went in and called out to him." He pauses. "I found him in his office." He gulps again. "There was a note." Josh rakes a hand through his dark hair. "Suicide."

My jaw drops and I feel like my eyes are bulging out of my head.

Travis doesn't say anything, simply turns on his heels and strides down the hallway where they took Harold.

I focus back on Josh. He's in jeans and button-down blue shirt, which compliments his eyes. Of course, his hair is a mess. He's always running his hands through it. I bend down in front of him and take his hands in mine. "I'm sorry," I say because it's all I can say. I can't tell him Harold will be ok because he might not be. Harold was like a second father to Josh. Taught him how to play chess. They were two quiet brooding buddies. I never understood their relationship, but Harold meant a lot to Josh and I'm pretty sure the feeling was mutual.

Josh pulls me to him.

I give him a half standing hug. It kills my back, but I would stay like this forever for Josh. I need to be his anchor like he's been mine for so many years. He loosens his hold and I bend back down to stare into his eyes.

Josh studies me for a moment then parts his lips and glances down at mine.

My heart flips. Is he thinking of kissing me?

Someone clears their throat behind me.

I stagger back and almost trip over the chair behind me.

Josh jumps up and catches me before I fall backward. Travis lunged for me too so I end up being held up by both of them. It's like the story of my life. Split between these two guys. I smile at each of them before distancing myself.

My heart is going crazy in my chest and my mind is still wondering if Josh was planning to kiss me. I push the thought aside because now is not the time to think about it.

I need to focus on Harold and the guy who says he's Eddie...and Regina. If she's not dead, where is she? Not to mention solve the cold case murders of Laura and her family. Ugh. This is a lot. What have I gotten myself into? It's like a complex web, which is somehow connected, but how?

Travis clears his throat again.

I blink. Travis and Josh are staring at me like they do when they know I've zoned out on them. I blush. "Sorry, just thinking."

Travis smirks. "Figures." He cuts his eyes to Josh then me and raises his eyebrow.

I narrow my eyes at him. He doesn't get to give me a hard time about Josh. It's none of his business. Besides, he's dating Allison, so why does he care if I kiss Josh? The thought of kissing Josh makes my heart speed up. What is going on with me? It must be nerves. I've never entertained the idea of being with Josh and I don't plan to start now...right?

"Autumn, are you alright? You're flushed," Violet asks, coming up next to me.

I notice the temperature in the room has definitely gone up, but I don't think it's because Laura's gone. I ignore her question and ask, "How's Eddie?" I don't know what else to call him so I guess I'm sticking with Eddie until further notice.

Her eyes fill with tears. "He's in intensive care. Dr. Gregory got the bullet out, but Eddie's vitals are all over the place. They're not sure he'll make it through the night." She bursts into tears and rushes into my arms.

I wrap my arms around her, although I'm a little surprised she's leaning on me for comfort when she's spent the summer glaring at me, but maybe we've turned a corner with everything going on. I lead her toward a chair and she collapses into it.

"I don't know what I'll do if anything happens to him. I-I love him," she sniffles.

My heart breaks for her. I'm not sure anything I can say will bring her comfort so I simply stay quiet and let her cry.

Travis shifts uncomfortably in front of us. Crying makes him nervous. He never knows what to do and just wants it to stop. Josh, on the other hand, has taken the chair next to Violet and is whispering softly to her. His deep voice seems to soothe her and her cries turn to whimpers.

"Autumn, can I see you for a moment?" Travis motions with his head to the corner by the nurse's station.

I pat Violet on the back and tell her I'll be right back. I'm not sure she heard me, but I get up and move toward Travis. I can feel Josh's eyes on my back. Normally, it wouldn't bother me because I know he's always looking out for me, but for some reason today, I glance back and send him a reassuring smile.

He seems surprised. His eyebrows shot to his hairline before quickly recovering and grinning back at me.

I turn back to find Travis leaning against the wall taking in the scene. He doesn't appear angry just resigned. That thought makes me anxious. In high school, it was always Travis and me. Planning our future. Our careers. Our wedding. Our children. Our life. A part of me still thinks about it, but then there's the part of me that isn't ready to move forward...with him. I push the thoughts away because really, Autumn, now is not the time to be thinking about the two men in your life or well, I guess just one now.

"Something you care to share?" Travis nods toward Josh, who has gone back to comforting Violet.

I shake my head because there's nothing to share. I could have been totally imagining Josh thinking about kissing me. He could have just been trying to ground himself and staring at my lips was grounding, right? I shake my head again. I need to stop thinking about kissing Josh. Ok, I'm stopping. "How's Harold?"

Travis eyes me for a moment then says, "He's in a coma. They're running a toxicology panel, but there was a bottle sleeping pills next to him."

I frown. "What did the note say?"

"It was vague. Something about not being able to live a lie anymore."

"Did it say what lie?"

"No. Like I said, it was vague."

I bite my lip. "Are you sure Harold wrote it?"

Now it was Travis's turn to frown. "Are you thinking Eddie...or whoever that is, did this?"

I balk. "Of course not. I don't think Eddie did any of this."

Travis scowls. "Autumn, we went over this. Walter is dead. That man in intensive care isn't him. He fed you a bunch of lies including everything that went down yesterday."

"What do you mean?"

He runs a hand through his hair and pulls me further away from the nurses' station. "The supplies for the bomb and the rats were all charged to Eddie's credit card."

"What about the text he got?"

"A burner phone, which we found inside his house."

"Someone could have planted it."

"He bought it, Autumn." Travis sighs. "We think he even set the fire, which was made to look like rats chewed the wires." He pauses. "They were cut and laid by some paper to catch fire. His house was also doused in gasoline, which is why it went up so quickly. Of course, you know his prints were found in Regina's car too." His eyes well up over for a moment before he blinks the tears away and swallows hard.

"So, if this guy isn't Walter, who is he?"

"Eddie Bell."

"Huh?"

"For all intense and purposes, this guy is Eddie Bell. Legally, anyway, but there's no record of an adoption or of him working in Chicago or even him going to law school. He didn't exist until he came to Daysville."

My mind spins with this information. "Someone is doing this."

"Autumn," Travis moans.

"Ask Violet. Remember when Walter fell out of the old apple tree by the playground in kindergarten?" I don't wait for him to answer before continuing, "He broke his arm and got some bark jammed into his leg. He had to get stitches and there's a scar. Violet saw it. Ask her, she'll tell you."

Travis runs a hand over his face. "It doesn't prove anything, Autumn."

I narrow my eyes at him. "What do you mean it doesn't prove anything? It proves Walter Smoot didn't die with his grandparents. It proves everything he's been telling us is true."

"Autumn, I can't." Travis stops talking when Allison waltzes in the door with Cat on her heels. He leaves me standing in the corner while he approaches his girls.

His girls. My stomach churns at the word.

Allison's face lights up when she sees him and she plants a kiss on his cheek.

Cat cringes, but not enough for Travis or Allison to catch it. She scans the waiting room until her eyes land on me. Her eyes brighten and she rushes over to me, throwing her arms around my waist. She bursts into tears.

I rub her back and feel my own tears falling down my cheeks.

Allison purses her lips while Travis takes us in with a look of longing, or maybe he's wishing Cat was hugging him.

I stroke Cat's auburn hair and try to get her to calm down. She's wailing now and people are glancing over at us with curious expressions.

Allison nudges Travis with her elbow and he snaps out of his trance.

He reaches us in a couple of strides and untangles Cat from my embrace although he doesn't seem very happy about it. Cat leans against him, using his shirt as a handkerchief. Travis doesn't appear to mind as he wipes her hair back from her face. He gives me a quick nod before turning from me.

Allison joins them and they take off toward the cafeteria.

I watch them go with a sense of longing in me. Cat could have been my daughter. Our daughter. Sometimes she feels like she is. My phone buzzes in my pocket, snapping me from my thoughts. I pull it from my scrub pocket and click on the text. It's from an unknown number.

I need your help. R.M.

14

"Where are we going?" Josh stares out at the dark road in front of us. There's nothing but cornfields on either side of us and I can't help but think we're heading into a trap.

After I got the text, Dr. Gregory came to get Violet and take her back to the intensive care to sit with Eddie. He thought if Eddie wasn't going to make it through the night, he would want to spend it with her. His words set Violet off into another bout of tears, which allowed me time to grab Josh and slip out unnoticed.

Now, we're headed...well, I'm not sure. I keep getting texts telling me where to turn. It's kind of eerie like someone is tracking my phone, which makes me wonder if we're heading into a trap. If there's any chance Regina is texting me, there's no way I can't go. R.M. stands for Regina Mills, right? I keep wondering if I should text Travis, but I have Josh so we'll be ok...I hope.

"Another left."

Josh turns down a dirt road and glances over at me. It's dark, but I know his face is etched with worry.

An old log cabin comes into view ahead of us. The windows are dark and it's totally creepy. I grip Josh's arm. "Do you think she's in there?"

"Let's hope it's just her."

Josh cuts the lights and turns off the engine. We sit in silence for a moment, listening for anything unusual. The crickets serenade us while we continue to stare at the house.

"Autumn." Josh grips my hand. "I think we should call Travis."

"Use your phone. I think mine's being tracked."

Josh holds up his phone. "No signal."

"Really?" I check mine and I don't have any signal either. Great. I should have called Travis earlier. "The sooner we go in and get Regina, the sooner we can go home."

"If we make it home," Josh mumbles.

I slap him in the chest. "Don't say stuff like that. We're going to make it home."

He nods and scans the area around the cabin before opening his door.

I do the same.

We meet at the hood of the Jeep. The night air is muggy and stale. A strange smell wafts through the air. It's a mixture of bleach and sandalwood.

A curtain moves in one of the windows.

"Someone's inside. Let's go." I move toward the front door, but Josh catches my arm.

"I'll go first. Stay behind me and if anything happens to me, you take the keys and get out of here."

I scoff. "I'm not leaving you."

He grabs my other arm and spins me to face him. "Promise me, Autumn." Even in the moonlight, his baby blues sparkle.

My breath catches and I glance at his lips before

nodding. What's wrong with me? I'm thinking about kissing Josh when Regina could be hurt or in danger. Heck, we could be in danger. Get your head in the game, Autumn.

Josh lets go of my arms and takes my hand. He leads me toward the front door, stopping every few seconds to listen to our surroundings.

My palms are sweaty and my heart is about to beat out of my chest. The unknown is killing me...well not really, but my anxiety is through the roof.

When we finally reach the front door, Josh reaches for the handle. He pushes it open and it's too dark to see inside.

"You came," Regina said, her voice sounding kind of faint and weak.

I push my way into the cabin and the door slams shut behind us. There's shuffling and then the cabin fills with light. I blink against it until my eyes can focus. There's a gray-haired, scrawny man, who looks kind of familiar standing in the corner next to the light switch. He's holding a gun on us. Regina is sitting on a twin bed in the opposite corner hooked up to some sort of IV. The IV is filled with fluids, but Regina doesn't look well. She's severely pale and her other arm is bruised. "What's going on?"

"Sit down, Autumn." She gestures to the dining room table in the middle of the room.

I scan the room and realize it's just one big room. The kitchen is pressed against the front wall, two twin beds on another wall, the dining room is in the middle and a couch and a couple chairs face a TV in another corner.

Josh flops down in a chair while I move to Regina and check her wounds.

She flinches when I run a hand over her bruises.

"What happened?"

Regina sighs and points at the wiry man in the corner. "Autumn, meet Dean Smoot."

I gasp. "Eddie's father?"

Dean lifts a gray eyebrow and clenches his jaw.

"I mean Walter."

His face softens and he nods.

"But you died...in a car accident."

He shakes his head.

I frown and turn to Regina. "I'm lost."

Regina takes a labored breath and lies back on the bed. "It's a long story, Autumn."

"Well, we're not going anywhere until you tell us. Right, Josh?" I cast a glimpse over at him

Josh gives me a curt nod then glares at Dean. He folds his arms across his chest in an attempt to be intimidating.

Regina sighs and closes her eyes, not saying anything for several minutes.

When I realize she's not going to talk, I ask, "Why are you framing Eddie or Walter for your murder?"

Her eyes fly open. "Wh-What are you talking about?"

"Travis arrested him for your murder." I eye her then Dean before continuing, "Your blood was found in your car along with his fingerprints and a taped confession from you stating you killed Eddie's family."

Regina gasps then chokes.

I grab the water by the bed and hold it up to her lips.

When she finally composes herself, she takes another deep breath and says, "We aren't framing Eddie...Walter."

"Then what's with the blood?" I gesture to her arms.

"Someone wants me dead. If they thought I was already dead, then they would stop hunting me."

"Who?"

"No clue."

Sheesh. Now, she sounds like Travis.

"When Eddie...Walter came back to town, I started getting threatening texts. Then when you joined in his hunt to find Laura's killer, they started threatening you. I got another text last Saturday."

"If I go down, you do too."

She sighs again. "You saw it. Did you see the ones before it?"

I shake my head. "Travis took it before I had a chance."

She bites her lip. "He's probably so confused. I never meant for any of this to get out of hand. He's been through so much already."

I nod. "What did the other texts say?"

"Just more threats to expose me, kill me and you." She squeezes my hand. "I got scared so I called Dean to pick me up outside of town. I left anything that could be tracked and hiked through the woods until I reached the service road. Dean picked me up and we came up with a plan."

"To fake your own death." I pause and glance at Dean. "It was you I saw driving Regina's car down Main Street, wasn't it?"

Dean nods.

"Why fake your death? Why not just tell Travis? He would have helped you."

Regina sighs again. "I'm in too deep, Autumn. I've been harboring Dean for years. I knew he faked his death and I didn't report it. Someone else must know too. That's why I'm being threatened."

"Travis would understand."

Regina shakes her head and tears fall down her cheeks. "He wouldn't," she whispers.

"Of course, he would. He would do anything for you." I squeeze her hand.

More tears stream down her face and she continues to shake her head.

Dean clears his throat. "I guess it's my turn to fill in the gaps."

"That would be nice," Josh mumbles.

I flash him a look and he shrugs.

"Laura and I moved to town after Eddie was born. I started working for the Holliday family. First, it was just yardwork then I was promoted to their driver. I heard stuff. Illegal stuff. Family secrets. Then one day, I overheard something I shouldn't have. The next day, they sent me on an errand and my brakes went out. I slammed into another car." He pauses and locks eyes with Regina. She lets out a sob and covers her mouth with her hand.

I glance back and forth between them, completely confused. "Am I missing something?"

Dean pulls his eyes from Regina's and stares down at the floor before muttering, "It was Travis's parents' car."

15

I gasp and Josh mumbles something under his breath.

Dean's voice cracks when he continues, "They died instantly. I was hurt but knew if I 'lived,' the Hollidays would just find another way to kill me. I left my clothes in the car, took the spare gas can out of the trunk and blew up the car." He runs a hand through his hair.

I blink and let his words sink in. Eddie's dad killed Travis's parents. How did I not know this? "Does Travis know?" I turn to Regina.

She shakes her head. "The Hollidays must have not wanted their name or their car linked to the accident so the report reads it was hit and run."

"And you've kept this from Travis? All these years?"

Regina squeezes my hand tighter as tears continue to run down her face. "I wanted to tell him. So many times, I wanted to, but by the time he was old enough to understand, I was in too deep. I couldn't tell him and not be punished for hiding Dean."

My head understands her logic, but my heart is loyal to Travis and I know this will break him. I tap down my feelings and turn to Dean. "So, you've just been living here for years? Illegally?"

"Laura's family owns this land. When she and her parents died, it was put in a trust for Wallie. He got access to it years ago and I expected him to show up and find me, but he never did. When he came back a few months ago, I thought for sure he was going to come out here, but he never has." He glances around the room. "This old cabin has been my home ever since the accident." He wipes a hand over his face. "I didn't know who I could trust since the Hollidays practically have every cop in their pocket. Heck, they altered the accident report because the Hollidays asked them too, what else would they do for them?" He runs a hand through his gray hair. "I didn't want to put Laura and Eddie in danger so I stayed away. Tried to fend for myself. I was dumpster diving shortly after my 'funeral' and Regina saw me. She offered to help me even after I..after-." His voice trails off, then he whispers, "Killed her brother and sister-in-law."

"It wasn't your fault," Regina pipes up, her voice filled with anger. "Those awful Hollidays are responsible for my family's deaths. For our pain. You didn't do anything wrong."

He grins at her. "You're a saint, Regina."

She waves him off, but I can see her blushing even in the low light.

"She brings me food and clothes, whatever I need them."

I glance over at Regina. Her face is really red.

Suddenly, the cabin turns ice cold.

Laura.

Rage consumes me and I can't catch my breath, but my voice comes out strong and fierce. "So, you left your family. Your wife...to die."

Reflexology & Revenge 99

Dean snaps his head back like I slapped him. "Wh-What?"

"Didn't you think for one second about your family?"

He glares at me. "Of course, I did. Every day."

Regina touches my arm, but I snatch it back. "Don't touch me," I hiss. "You helped him. Helped him abandon his family." I study her. "You always loved him. Wanted him for yourself. That's why you were so eager to help him. Keep him all to yourself out here in the middle of nowhere while his family suffered."

She gasps and her eyes fill with tears.

Josh gapes at me. "Autumn? You don't sound like yourself. Are you alright?"

I ignore him and turn back to Dean. "Your wife died because she wouldn't tell him where it is and he didn't want her ratting on him. Then he killed her parents to ensure his secrets were safe and left Wallie an orphan. He had to go live with that snooty family in Chicago. They even renamed him, Eddie. Eddie Bell." I glare at him. "You could have stepped up. Told the police everything you knew. Rescued my sweet boy." I drop to my knees, my hands pressed to my chest and I rock back and forth like I'm holding a baby. Tears are falling from my eyes, but I know they're not mine.

Dean crouches down next to me. "Your sweet boy?"

I stare at him and his eyes register something.

"Laura?"

I nod.

"How? Why? What?" He rakes a hand through his gray hair. "How is this possible?"

I shrug.

"I'm sorry. I was young. Scared. I didn't know they were going to go after you or your parents. I thought by leaving, I was keeping you safe. Keeping Wallie safe. I'm so sorry." He pulls me into his arms and we weep together.

A light flashes across the windows and instantly Laura leaves me. I shift to move away from Dean.

"She's gone?"

I nod.

He drops his arms and wipes his eyes.

Josh is frowning and so is Regina.

A car door shuts outside.

Dean grabs his gun, snuffs out the lanterns and ducks behind the door.

Josh grabs my hand and we stumble our way in the dark behind the twin bed.

I grasp Regina's hand and she squeezes back. I'm glad she's not mad at me. It was like Laura took over my mind and body. I can't say I'm a fan of letting someone control my actions and words, but I think Laura needed the closure.

Footsteps sound on the porch. Light from a flashlight moves across the windows. The knob on the door turns and a dark figure pushes open the door.

Dean jumps out from behind the door and slams the butt of his gun on their head.

The person goes down in a heap on the floor.

Someone screams from the porch.

"Cat?" I hurry out from behind the bed and take the shaking teenager in my arms. "What are you doing here?"

"Daddy tracked your phone."

Travis groans on the floor, holding his head. "I told you to wait in the car, young lady."

Cat snorts. "When he couldn't find you and since you weren't answering your phone, he knew you were in trouble."

"I have no cell service. How could he track me?"

Travis moans again. "I may have put a tracking device on your phone battery after the last case." He cracks an eye to see my reaction while he holds his head.

I narrow my eyes at him and try to act angry, but I'm having a hard time refraining from smiling. He still cares about me. Even if he's dating someone else. The thought warms my heart.

He smirks at me then grabs the back of the chair and hoists himself up with Dean's help. "Who are you?"

"Long story," Regina drawls.

"Aunt Regina?" Cat squeals, but no one can see much of anything with Travis's flashlight.

Dean moves away from Travis and turns on the lanterns. Light fills the cabin and everyone begins talking and hugging.

Regina tells Travis everything while Cat and I tend to her wounds. Josh even rubs her feet to help her relax while we change her bandages.

Travis stands next to her bed with a stoic expression, which says he's not happy about any of this. "Dean, what did you overhear?" He turns to the spot where Dean was hanging back to give us space. "Dean?"

I look up from my wound care and the cabin's empty. The front door is wide open and Dean's gone. "Where did he go?"

"Maybe he went outside to get some air." Regina shifts and tries to sit up to search for him.

Travis motions for Josh to come with him. "Let's check around the house."

I finish bandaging Regina and give her some more water.

When they come back, Travis is shaking his head. "He's gone."

16

I shift in the pew next to Josh. My black dress is stifling me. Why? Because I hate funerals. No. Eddie didn't die. Thank goodness. He's recovering quite nicely. Dr. Gregory is amazed by his progress and thinks he'll be released next week as long as he doesn't get an infection. He's also confirmed to be Walter Smoot after a tech found a glitch in the computer system. So, he's been cleared of all charges, even the shooting.

Strangely, the captain is saying it was all a misunderstanding. Supposedly, Eddie tripped, making it look like he was lunging for the gun. The captain released a press statement taking full responsibility for the shooting and asking for Eddie's forgiveness, which he gave. So, the captain gets to keep his job, must to my dismay.

Violet hasn't left Eddie's side so we're listening to the Crafty Crew ladies bellowing, *Amazing Grace* without any piano music. It's like listening to a bunch of frogs croaking in a pond, but the old gals are belting it out like they're Beyonce's backup singers so I refrain from plugging my ears.

Harold is on display a few feet in front of them. His gray

suit is pressed and his wiry gray hair is plastered to his head. He doesn't look like himself at all. I glare over at his brothers dressed in dark suits, their gray heads bowed like they're mourning. Maybe they are, I'm sure they loved Harold, but they were quick to take him off life support on Tuesday morning. Of course, Dr. Gregory informed them Harold was brain dead, but they didn't even think about it before pulling the plug.

Judge Holliday also released a statement this week. Only his was heartbreaking. Apparently, Harold left him a letter confessing to everything. He planted the bomb, the rats, orchestrated the break-in and shooting, erased Eddie's background and even hacked into his accounts. I guess Harold was a computer genius, with mad hacking skills. Who knew? He also confessed to framing Eddie, when he found all the blood in Regina's car. How he got Eddie's fingerprints in her car, I guess no one will ever know. He even made the recording of Regina confessing to the murders by splicing together conversations he had with her about Eddie. I guess the guy recorded everything. He also sent Regina the threatening texts.

So, why'd sweet Harold do all of this? According to the note, which no one has seen but Judge Holliday and the police, Harold murdered Laura Smoot because she stole something precious of his and wouldn't tell him where it was. He thought maybe she hid it at her parents', but they acted like they didn't know anything so they had to go too.

When Eddie came back to town, Harold got scared. In all his paranoia, he somehow thought Regina knew he killed Laura and her parents so he followed her, planning to kill her when he discovered Dean was still alive and she was helping him. So, he threatened to expose her to keep from going to jail. It all got to be too much for him so he decided to end his life.

Guess that's it. Case closed.

I'm not buying it for a second and neither is Eddie. It all seems too convenient. Blaming the dead guy so the real killer can go free. I have my suspicions on who the real killer is, but I need more proof.

Josh sniffles and wipes his eyes with a handkerchief. He's been more quiet than normal over the past few days. I know he's grieving and it breaks my heart.

A tear slips from my eye and I wipe it away. My eyes begin to burn and I try to keep from rubbing them. I'm still not used to these gel orbs in my eyes. Yes. I made it to my eye appointment and was in dire need of glasses or contacts. I opted for contacts because I'm not sure I'm ready for glasses. I have a pair in my nightstand just in case my contacts and I decide to break up, but so far, we seem to be getting along just fine.

It's Friday and we've spent the week swamped at the spa. People were booking appointments more for gossip then reflexology or massage, but at least we were busy. We've also been tending to Regina. After searching for Dean for several hours and not finding him, we gave up and took Regina to the hospital. She had to have a blood transfusion after faking her own death but is doing well.

Travis is working with Judge Holliday and Regina's attorney to get her out of several charges including faking her own death and harboring Dean after he faked his death all those years ago. Dean will be in trouble too when they find him, but so far, he's MIA. Travis thinks he's skipped town and we'll never see him again, but I think he's still close.

Laura's been MIA too since the encounter with Dean.

I've visited the red room several times over the past few days and she's ghosting me. No pun intended. I've even questioned Regina about the wall between the red room and her salon. She tells me she has no clue, but I can tell she's still keeping something from me.

A flash of red slipping into the pew across from me catches my attention. Travis. He slips an arm around Allison and I have to bite my lip to keep from gasping. Not that I should be surprised. They're dating. We've been tiptoeing around the subject the past few days when he's stopped by to visit Regina. Now, isn't the time to deal with personal matters. Our focus is on the case and Regina.

I think back to our suspect list. Basically, the whole suspect list is seated in the first pew. Judge Holliday is on the end. He looks so much like Harold, it's eerie. Next to him is his brother, Dave then there's Captain Rivers and lastly, the fire chief, Bob Billings.

I'm not taking Harold off the list yet because something tells me he played a part in all of this, but I'm not sure exactly how. His suicide seems a little too convenient. According to Josh, Harold didn't take anything but supplements. He hated any sort of pharmaceutical drugs. So where did the sleeping pills come from?

Preacher John motions for all of us to stand and we sing the last hymn before following the coffin out of the church. I follow Josh out of the pew and almost run smack into Travis, who is coming out of his pew across from me. He smirks and opens his mouth to say something when Allison hooks her arm in his and plasters herself against his side. My stomach churns as I send the happy couple a quick smile and hurry after Josh.

The late afternoon sun is beating down on the pavement and we could probably fry an egg on it. Judge Holiday and

Dave follow the coffin while everyone else heads to their vehicles. They wanted a private burial so the town's not invited.

I step to the side to watch the brothers and let Travis and Allison pass, but Allison decides to reel me in with a line of questions.

"Autumn, how are you? Isn't this so sad? Can you believe Harold would do such a thing?"

I give her another tight-lipped smile and say, "Harold was a sweet soul. It's truly a loss for Daysville."

Allison gives me a sad smile and flips her red hair over her slender shoulder that's covered by a cap-sleeve. Her black dress is clinging to her petite frame and she really could be a runway model.

Travis adjusts his tie and Allison's hand slips out from his arm. She seems a little taken aback by the action, but recovers quickly. "Are you going over to Pete's after this? It's so sweet of him to open early and give everyone a free slice of pizza since the Hollidays aren't hosting a dinner." She scoffs and lowers her voice. "I can't believe they had Harold's funeral so late in the day. Probably did it so they wouldn't have to feed everyone. For being one of the richest families in town, they sure are cheap."

"I'm actually going to head home."

"Hot date?" Allison winks at me.

I fight the urge to roll my eyes, but then smile and respond, "Actually, yes."

Travis jerks slightly at my comment. I wish he didn't have his aviators on because I would love to see his eyes right now. My guess is they're bugging out of his head.

I know I shouldn't mess with him, but seeing him with Allison is bringing out a petty side of me.

Allison doesn't seem to notice his stiff posture and practically squeals with delight. "Oh, I didn't know you were dating anyone. Who is it? Where are you going?" She claps her hands together like I just showed her a magic trick.

"To the Luke Bryan concert tonight."

She squeals again. "We're going too. We should double date."

Travis shifts uncomfortably next to her and says, "Allison, we don't want to intrude on their date."

She waves him off then pauses. "Oh, gosh. Is this a first date? Travis is probably right we wouldn't want to intrude, but be sure to introduce us. K." she says as Travis tugs her toward his SUV.

I smile and wave to her.

"What was that?"

I jump and spin around. "Josh, don't sneak up on me."

He arches an eyebrow. "Hot date? I thought you were going with Nikki to the concert."

I smirk at him. "Nikki's hot."

He snorts. "You do realize they are going to see you at the concert with Nikki and no guy, right?"

I bite my lip. I didn't really think this through. I was just trying to get under Travis's skin. Now, I'm going to look like a pathetic liar. Maybe I can cancel on Nikki. I need to work on finding out what Dean heard that led to a series of murders and cover-ups and if Laura did take something, what was it and where is it?

As if Josh can read my mind, he says, "Don't even think about canceling on Nikki. She texted me threatening me physical harm if you even hint at bailing. Bobby is going to be there and she needs backup."

I groan. "Why don't those two just figure it out already? I feel like this is high school all over again."

Josh frowns. "Gosh, I hope not."

I bump his shoulder. "I thought you liked high school."

"The only thing I liked about high school was seeing you all day."

His words cause me to blush and I tuck a strand of hair behind my ear. "You see me all day, every day, now."

He shakes his head. "Not really. We're like ships passing in the night. Always going in with clients or chasing bad guys. I feel like we don't really get to hang out and talk anymore. You spent the summer working with Eddie so I rarely saw you." He lowers his voice to almost a whisper, "I miss you."

Guilt hits me like a tidal wave and my heart cracks. I blink back tears. "I'm sorry." I tuck my arm in his as we head toward the Jeep. "How about once we solve this case, we take a trip together?"

"Really?" His voice raises slightly with excitement as he opens my door.

"Really." I slip in and stare out at him.

He leans against the door and grins at me. His eyes slip to my lips for a split second, causing my heart to skip. He smiles and shuts the door.

What's happening? Josh is my best friend. Period. I need to shut down these feelings. I roll down the window to get some fresh air even if it's hot air.

Shouts from the graveyard have me pushing open my door and running in heels across the scorching pavement. I stop just short of the graveyard and Josh almost runs into my back.

"Sorry," he mumbles.

I pat his shoulder to reassure him I'm fine then take in the scene in front of me.

The Holliday brothers are in a heated argument while the captain tries to separate them.

"He's dead because of you," Dave yells at Judge Holliday and clocks him in the jaw.

Judge Holliday staggers back, his hand flying to his cheek. "You- ungrateful punk." He lunges for Dave, who doesn't cower but puts up his fist to fight.

"Harold was sick and you refused to get him help." Dave punches the Judge in the stomach and he drops to his knees. Dave goes in to punch him again, but the captain grabs his arms and holds them behind his back.

The judge gets to his feet and pulls his arm back like he's going to sucker punch his brother in the stomach when he spots Josh and me. He says something to Dave and the captain before they take off toward the captain's cruiser and the judge makes his way over to us. Even in his sixties, the man still has an air of confidence about him. His strides are precise and calculated. He's slender and tall like Harold. The only difference is the judge's gray hair, which is combed to one side whereas Harold's was always wiry and standing up. "Autumn. Josh. Sorry for the commotion. Dave's just upset. As you know, Josh, Harold was depressed for some time."

Josh stiffens beside me but doesn't say anything.

"Lately, he'd been a little more agitated. We should have pushed for him to get help. That's what Dave meant when he accused me." He studies me like he's trying to determine if I believe him.

I smile and nod. "Of course, we just wanted to make sure everything was alright. I know Harold had a tough road. I'm sure it was heartbreaking seeing him go off to the psychiatric hospital when he was so young."

Judge Holliday frowns and shakes his head. "What do you mean, Miss Fisher. Harold has never been to any psychiatric hospital."

"Really? I could have sworn I saw a picture of him in the newspaper archives."

His face pales and he straightens. "You must be mistaken."

I open my mouth to tell him I'm not when Josh grips my waist, pulling me into his side. "We're very sorry for your loss, your honor."

He reaches for Josh's hand and clasps it. "I appreciate that, Mr. Parker. Harold always spoke fondly of you. He really enjoyed your chess matches." He gives Josh's hand a squeeze before withdrawing his and saying, "Well, I better go check on Dave. Have a nice night."

We watch him head over to the black limo parked next to the graveyard.

"Why did you interrupt me?"

Josh shakes his head. "Today isn't the day to pry."

Guilt seeps in and I want to berate myself for my lack of tact. It's Harold's funeral for goodness sakes, Autumn. I'm so focused on solving this case, I'm losing all sense of human decency and empathy. Sheesh.

"Let's go." Josh still has his arm around my waist and tugs lightly to move me toward the Jeep.

I sigh, wishing I could put all the pieces together and solve this case for Laura, Eddie, Dean, Regina and even Harold.

Josh gives my hip a squeeze as if reading my thoughts. "You'll figure it out, Autumn. You always do."

I glance over my shoulder and notice the Judge watching me. A chill runs down my spine. "Let's hope I do before it's too late."

17

Nikki screams next to me and I jump. She grins at me. "I can't wait for Luke to get out here. Sam Hunt was so good. I just love him," she gushes. Her long dark hair is cascading down her back and her green sundress matches her eyes, which are shining in the stage lights. We have front row tickets and even had meet and greet passes. "Let's go get something to drink before he comes on." She grabs my hand and leads me through the crowd of people. Our cowboy boots click on the ramp as we make our way to the vendors. The faint smell of cow manure mixed with fresh popcorn and beer hits us as approach the small snack stand behind the bleachers. Nikki tucks her arm in mine and asks, "Are you having fun? You seem a little distracted tonight."

"I'm having fun, but yes, I'm a little preoccupied. Sorry." I shoot her a smile and tuck a strand of loose hair behind my ear. My side French braid is falling out from all the dancing. I opted for cut off jean shorts and a flowy blue top with my leather cowboy boots. There's a slight breeze tonight, but with all the people it's not helping keep anyone cool.

"Nikki! Autumn!" Allison rushes over to us, dragging Travis with her. She is a vision in a short floral dress and cowboy boots with her hair twisted in a bun on top of her head while Travis looks like a rugged cowboy in jeans and a short sleeve white t-shirt. "Where are your dates? I've been watching for you guys all night." Allison glances around like she could conjure them with her eyes.

Bobby picks that time to join us and slips an arm around Nikki's waist. "Everyone having a good time?" He gazes down at Nikki with those big brown eyes. Then he mouths. "I'm sorry."

She melts and mouths, "Me too." Then snuggles up to his broad chest and loops a thumb through his jeans belt loop. Her other hand splays across his black t-shirt with the words, Farmers Rock, on the front. And just like that their fight is over. This really is like high school all over again.

"We're having so much fun, aren't we babe?" Allison pecks Travis on the cheek and wraps an arm around him.

Ugh. I may vomit with all the cutesy couples and their PDA.

She peeks around Bobby and asks, "Autumn, where's your date?"

My stomach drops and starts to churn even more. Maybe I can act like I'm going to throw up and then just leave. No. Nikki will follow me. Travis will come to check on me. It's nice having friends who care about me, but right now I could use a little less caring. Guess it's time to come clean. I open my mouth to explain myself when someone grabs my arm and twirls me into their chest. Strong hands go to my hips while my hands splay out against mounds of muscle covered by gray fabric. A hand tilts my chin up to meet his eyes. Familiar blue eyes and the smell of tea tree and mint consume me.

"There you are," he says and leans down to brush a light kiss to my lips.

I may faint. My knees buckle and Josh tightens his hold on me. His touch lights my skin on fire. What's happening? This is Josh. I can feel my skin flush. It's a good thing it's dark because I would probably look like a tomato right now. I gaze up at him and he winks at me then leans down and whispers in my ear, "I couldn't let you make a fool of yourself." Then he kisses my cheek. Two kisses from Josh in one night. I'm not sure my heart can handle it. I touch my cheek where his lips just were, then realize we have an audience.

Nikki's jaw is almost on the ground. Bobby's smirking next to her. Allison looks about ready to burst with excitement while Travis's fists are clenched at his sides and his jaw is tight. He's glaring at me and I can practically feel the anger rolling off him.

"Oh. My. Gosh!" Allison shrieks, drawing gazes from people walking by. "When did this happen? I mean I always suspected, even gossiped about it, but you two always insisted you were just friends. Best friends." She smacks Travis in the chest, but he doesn't even flinch. "See, I told you this would happen."

He mumbles something I can't make out then turns and pulls Allison away from us. She protests for a moment then gives in and waves over her shoulder. I'm sure the whole town will know about this before the end of Luke's first song.

I sigh then realize I'm still tucked into Josh's side. I move away slightly and hear him scoff.

Nikki tackles me and Josh, dragging us into a group hug. "This is so great! I'm so happy for you guys. Now, we can go on double dates." She lets us go and starts rambling about everything we can all do together. Couples retreats. Couples massages. Couples yoga.

I open my mouth to tell her the truth before she gets too ahead of herself with all this couples stuff, but Luke comes out on stage.

Nikki and Bobby take off to the front row at my insistence.

I give Bobby my ticket and hang back with Josh. "Did you buy a ticket?"

He digs in his jeans and shows me his ticket.

I smile at him. "You hate country music."

"True, but I love you and you needed me."

I flush and tuck another strand behind my ear. "You didn't have to, I would have just told them the truth."

He shrugs. "Figured you needed some good publicity since everyone was giving you such a hard time about helping Eddie when he was being accused of killing Regina."

I smirk. "And you're good publicity?"

He smiles. "Always."

I groan and bump his shoulder. "You're getting a big head in your old age Mr. Parker."

He laughs and throws an arm around me. "Want to go to my seats in the bleachers?"

I shake my head. "I won't subject you to this anymore. You've done enough for me tonight." I touch my lips, which still tingle from our kiss.

"It was my pleasure." He winks at me. "Come on."

I smile and follow him to his seats. "What are we going to tell everyone?"

"Let's not worry about that tonight." He takes my hand and twirls me out and into his chest then whispers in my ear, "Tonight, we dance."

I giggle because this is so unlike him. Josh doesn't dance. Not that he can't, he can, he's really good at it, but he just doesn't. He spins me again before climbing toward our seats. To my surprise, Josh actually bought two tickets so we could sit together. Unfortunately, they're right next to Travis and Allison.

Allison bounces up and down and claps her hands. "You two are so cute. I love your dance moves." She nudges Travis. "See, Josh dances. Why don't you?"

I cringe. Travis hates dancing. In his defense, he's awful at it. My feet throb at the memory of how many times he stepped on my toes at prom. "You're more than welcome to dance with Josh," I offer, not thinking she'll take me up on it, but she does.

She sways slightly as she makes her way across Travis and me to stand by Josh. The bleachers aren't the greatest place to dance, but we're on the end so there's a small platform where Josh gives her a little spin. She laughs and continues to dance by Josh.

I sneak a peek at Travis, who has his arms crossed and his eyes focused on the stage. "I'm surprised you're here."

He doesn't look at me, but asks, "Why?"

"Thought maybe you'd be covered up with paperwork at the station."

He grunts but doesn't say anything.

"Any leads on what Laura stole from Harold?"

Travis sighs. "Nope."

"Any reason to believe Harold was -," I pause and scan the bleachers for eavesdroppers before whispering, "Murdered?"

He scoffs. "Nope."

Well, so much for getting any information out of Travis. The guy probably won't ever say more than one word to me from now on. Way to go, Autumn, burning bridges after you just rebuilt them.

Sigh.

"You could have told me," Travis growls in my ear.

I play dumb. "Told you what?"

He snorts and gestures to Josh, who is spinning a beaming Allison around again. "About you two. I thought you two were just 'best friends.'" Guess not, huh?"

I ignore his question because I just found out about Josh and me. Not that there is a Josh and me… right? Plus, I can't tell him the truth. Not after Josh went to all the trouble of buying tickets and staging that gallant gesture. My heart flutters at the memory, but I stamp it down. Josh was just helping me. There's nothing romantic between us. We're friends. Best friends. Right?

"Autumn?

"Why didn't you tell me about Allison?" I retort.

He flinches then asks, "So, this is payback?"

I scoff. "Of course, not. I just…well, we haven't really talked all summer so I didn't think it was important."

Travis snorts. "You spent the summer holed up with Eddie Bell."

"So, you were jealous of Eddie and decided to ask out Allison?" I motion to the swaying redhead.

Travis clamps a hand over my mouth and shoots a glance at Allison, who is so wrapped up in the music there's no way she heard me. "Keep your voice down."

I bite his finger.

He yelps and yanks his hand back. "Ouch, what was that for?"

"For being an idiot."

"I'm an idiot. What did I do?" He asks, shaking his finger.

I open my mouth to tell him when his phone lights up in his hand.

Cat.

18

He answers and mumbles something I can't hear over the music. "I've got to go." He tries to squeeze by me, but I block him.

"What's wrong?"

"It's not any of your concern." He makes another attempt to get past me, but I don't let him. "Autumn, move."

"No. If it has anything to do with Regina, I'm going with you." I cross my arms and jut out my chin in defiance.

He sighs and motions for me to head out.

I whisper to Josh that there's an emergency. He offers to go with me, but I motion to Allison, who is still swaying and singing to the music. He nods and gives my hand a squeeze. I wait for Travis at the bottom of the bleachers while he deals with Allison. It's dark, but with the glow of the stage lights, she doesn't look too upset that Travis is leaving her with Josh. A part of me wonders if she's really into Travis or more into running the salon. Is Travis a stepping stone to get Regina to let her take over the salon? I shake my head. I'm being silly. Who wouldn't be into Travis?

Travis joins me at the bottom of the bleachers and

gestures to the field where the cars are parked. "I'm toward the back. It shouldn't be too hard to get out."

We make it to his SUV in a few minutes. I don't dare ask him what is going on until we're on the road headed back to Daysville. Villsboro, where the concert was being held is about a twenty-minute drive. Luke Bryan serenades us quietly from the radio speakers. I don't push Travis to talk to me. I mean I did just bite the guy. What was I thinking? He makes me so angry sometimes. Who does he think he is giving me a hard time for dating Josh and not telling him? Well, I'm not really dating Josh so I shouldn't be upset, but for some reason I am. He didn't tell me about Allison. I take a breath and try to calm myself down. I'm getting myself all worked up and I need to be focusing on the case.

"Cat says Dean's visiting Regina."

I gasp.

"She went to grab some dinner and when she came back Dean was in the room talking to Regina."

"So, he's still there?"

Travis frowns. His eyes are on the dark road ahead. "Maybe. I doubt it, but at least we know he hasn't skipped town."

"Did you call it in?"

He purses his lips and glares at me. "Of course, I did, but there's a disturbance at Harold's Hardware store so every cop is dealing with it right now."

"What kind of disturbance?"

"People are mad at Harold for everything he did. They're looting his store."

I gasp again. "That's awful. Our town is really deteriorating." I shake my head then ask, "Do you really believe Harold did all those things?"

He sighs. "It doesn't matter what I believe, Autumn. The evidence speaks for itself. Everything traces back to Harold."

"Maybe he's being framed?"

"Autumn," His tone is low and warning like.

"What? We've known Harold for years. Do you really think he's capable of killing an entire family? Over some sort of possession? Harold wasn't materialistic. He practically gave everything he owned away. I think he may have owned three outfits total."

"Maybe it was something sentimental. Something priceless that Laura stole. I would kill over that."

I roll my eyes even though he can't see me in the dark car. "You would never kill intentionally. I know you. Just like I know Harold. Something's off about this case."

Travis doesn't say anything for a few minutes then says, "If I dig into it, will you promise to keep your nose out of it?"

Before I can answer Travis's phone lights up with Cat's picture again. He answers and mutters a few words then hangs up.

"Dean's gone and Regina is pretending like he was never there." Travis grips the wheel, causing his knuckles to go white. "Why is she protecting him? The man's a murderer."

I can hear the pain in his voice. I reach out and place a hand on his thigh. "I'm sorry...about your parents."

Travis swallows, his Adam's apple bobbing up and down. "I can't believe she's been helping him all these years...still helping him." The hurt in his voice is palpable.

"Did you ask her?"

He frowns and shakes his head.

I bite my lip, contemplating if I should tell Travis about the picture Eddie found. "Travis, have you ever considered Regina's in love with Dean?"

His jaw drops and his eyes snap over to me before immediately going back to the road. "You're joking, right? Please tell me you are, although it's not funny, Autumn."

"Eddie found a picture of Regina glaring at Laura and Eddie. Laura even tol-," I stop, remembering how Travis doesn't believe in ghosts.

"Laura? Eddie's mother? Were you just going to say 'told?'" Travis runs one hand through his red hair and squeezes the wheel with the other. "You're talking about a ghost, right? You've seen Laura's ghost?"

I shrug.

"You know I don't believe in that paranormal stuff, Autumn."

"I know," I whisper and stare down at my hands.

Travis mutters something under his breath then lets out an exasperated breath. "If you did 'see' Laura, hypothetically, of course...what did she say?"

"She accused Regina of loving Eddie and wanting her out of the way."

Travis stares straight ahead and doesn't say anything for a few more minutes.

Daysville's city population sign comes into view, it hasn't been updated in several years, so according to the sign, we have one thousand three hundred and thirty-six people living in Daysville. I'm sure we've grown slightly over the past few years, but we're still a pretty small town. Too small to be dealing with all these murders.

"Show me."

"Show you what?"

"Laura."

I gape at him. "What do you mean?"

"Take me to where you have seen her and let me talk to her."

"It doesn't always work like that."

"Huh?"

"Well, I first saw her in the red room at the spa. It was right after Eddie moved to town. The room has always been hot or freezing cold. Doors stick. Stuff moves, but I never saw her until Eddie came to town." I pause and wonder if I should tell him about her taking over my body. "She showed me how she died. She was shot in the back...didn't see her killer."

He clenches his jaw but doesn't say anything.

"She showed up at Eddie's when he passed out from all the blood. I felt her."

His gaze snaps over to me. "What do you mean you felt her?"

"I mean we're somehow connected. I felt what she was feeling. Really cold. Really anxious. Couldn't breathe."

"So, it wasn't a panic attack?"

I shake my head. "Well, not mine, at least."

"Any place else she showed up?"

"At the hospital and then again at the cabin. That's where she confronted Regina."

"And since then?"

"MIA. Nothing."

"Well, it won't hurt to try and coax her out, will it?"

Travis makes a sharp left and heads to the spa.

19

"Come out. Come out. Wherever you are!"

I smack Travis in the gut and he huffs. "It doesn't work like that." We've been standing in the red room for the past thirty minutes. I tried to get Travis to head to the hospital and talk to Regina, but he sent another officer instead. He felt this took precedence over interrogating his aunt about her presumed crush, Dean Smoot and what he was doing visiting her in the hospital.

I personally think Travis is avoiding her. Their relationship has been a little strained over the past week, but I hope they can move past it. Travis doesn't need to lose anyone else in his life. Guilt threatens to rise to the surface again and I knock it down. He hasn't lost me. I'm right here. Standing in the creepy room waiting for Laura to show her face or her shadowy figure, whichever, I'm not picky as long as she makes an appearance.

"When you saw her, did she say or do anything?"

"She pointed at the wall." I gesture to the red wall.

Travis walks over and starts running his hand up and down the wall. "Regina told me she and Vicky never remodeled this part of the building. There's a supporting beam here so they just left it. He starts pushing until he finds a soft spot. "I think I found something. Do you have a hammer?"

"A ham-mer?" I stammer. "You're not seriously considering..." My words trail off because there's no way I'm letting him tear into the wall. How will I explain the repairs to Sally, especially if he doesn't find anything?"

"Autumn, a hammer. Come on.

I glare at him before snagging a hammer off the shelf and handing it to him.

He smacks the drywall, making a nice size hole in it. Surprisingly, it caves in easily. Travis sticks his hand in the hole and feels around. "There's a shelf in here, something's hanging from it. Do you have a flashlight?"

"A shelf?" I grab a flashlight off the shelf. Good thing we use this room for our storm shelter/storage. Everything Travis is asking for is within reach. I kneel down next to him and shine the light in the hole. "I don't see anything."

He removes his arm and takes the light. "Ah, I can't get the right angle to see what's stuck. I'm going to have to tear into the wall more."

I groan as he slams the hammer into the wall again. The drywall crumbles like a sandcastle, revealing a black velvet pouch hanging on a peg. "Well, that's not normal."

"Someone did a poor patch job."

"Someone like Laura."

At the mention of her name the room turns frigid and the overhead lights go out. Only the light from the flashlight shines in the dark room. I glance over my shoulder but don't see her. "She's here."

Travis nearly drops the hammer spinning around to catch a glimpse of her. "Where? I don't see her."

"I don't either."

He glares at me and shines the flashlight in my face. "Are you messing with me?"

"Hey." I hold up my hands to block the light. "Don't you feel how cold it is? Remember Josh's house? How it went from warm to cold."

He lowers the flashlight and nods slowly.

"Laura was there."

His eyes widen at the realization then he glances around the room again. "Why won't she show herself?"

I shrug. "Maybe she doesn't like you."

Travis narrows his eyes at me before turning back to the wall and removing the pouch. He opens it carefully and tips the contents into his hand.

"Pennies? Laura was murdered over pennies?"

Travis sets down the bag and holds a penny under the light to examine it, flipping it over and then back again. He frowns as if in deep concentration. "This is a rare 1964 Lincoln Cent SMS, which is worth about five grand a pop."

"I forgot what a coin nerd you are," I tease, rolling my eyes.

He ignores me and picks up another penny. His eyes widen. "This one is a 1964 D Penny."

"So, what. Travis focus." I snap my fingers, but he continues to study the penny. "These are pennies. Maybe valuable ones, but there's only like ten pennies here. Ten pennies here at five grand a pop is only a fifty grand. I know the Holliday family wouldn't kill for fifty grand. Harold was loaded, even though you'd never know it."

"Autumn, these aren't just any pennies. These are extremely rare. This D Penny is worth almost three point eight billion dollars."

My jaw drops and I feel light headed. "You're joking, right?"

Travis shakes his head. "Harold must have been a collector."

I bite my lip. "I never saw Harold with any coins. He loved rare chess pieces and don't get me started on his love for tools, but he never once showed us any coins."

He shrugs like it's no big deal and picks up another coin.

"Don't you think it's strange?"

"What?"

"That Harold never showed us his coin collection."

"Laura stole it." He gestures to the pennies.

I frown and the room gets colder. "Harold was obsessed with his chess pieces and his tools. He told me story after story about times as a child he would find a chess piece and save his money so he could buy it or how he'd find an old unique tool in abandoned barns."

"So?"

"So, Harold was obsessive-compulsive. He wouldn't just stop collecting pennies. He couldn't even if he wanted too. There were so many times where he'd show Josh and I a new tool or chess piece and say, *"I just couldn't help myself. I was compelled to buy it."*

"What are you getting at Autumn?"

"What if these pennies aren't Harold's?"

"Then who do they belong to?"

"Charles."

20

"You think these pennies belong to Judge Holliday?"

I nod. "Think about it, Travis. Harold and Charles are twins, right?"

Travis nods slowly, his frown deepening.

"What if they didn't share just looks, but also personality traits?"

"So, you think Charles, Judge Holliday, the most respected man in Daysville and one of the best judges I know, collected these coins, was obsessed over these coins and killed for them?" He pauses then continues, "So Laura steals them, he finds out, threatens her, but she won't tell him where they are so he kills her then proceeds to take a trip to Daysville a few months later and threatens her parents because he believes Laura gave them to her parents for safe keeping. When they don't tell him where they are, he kills them too." He eyes me then says, "He kills an entire family because he has an obsessive-compulsive personality, which caused him to be focused on nothing else but these coins."

My cheeks flush. "I know it sounds ridiculous, but you

should have seen the way Harold obsessed over his chess pieces and tools. He was always cleaning them. Even talked to them. They were his reason for living."

Travis raises an eyebrow and lets out an exasperated sigh. "Autumn, it's an interesting theory, but I know Judge Holliday and I've never seen him obsess about anything other than upholding the law. These coins had to have been stolen. The Hollidays don't have enough money to purchase all of these coins." He holds up the bag. "Judge Holliday wouldn't steal and he definitely wouldn't kill for these coins no matter how much they're worth. The guy releases bugs from his office out the window for goodness sakes."

I sigh. "Fine. If not Judge Holliday, then who?"

He opens his mouth when his phone rings. When he answers, wailing comes through the line. "Cat? Calm down. What's wrong?" He pauses while she screeches something unintelligible for a minute then Travis tells her to stay put and hangs up.

"What's wrong?"

"Regina's gone."

"What?" I shriek.

"She asked Cat to go get her some pudding from the cafeteria and when she came back, Regina was gone."

I glance at the coins. "Do you think..."

"What?"

I gesture to the coins.

Travis glares at me so hard, if this were a Disney movie, I would be stone right now. "Don't say anything you can't take back, Autumn. There's no way Regina would steal a bunch of coins and then kill for them."

"They're worth a lot of money, Travis. Money Regina didn't have after your parents died. Raising a child takes a lot of money and she was just getting her business off the ground. Maybe she and Laura stole the coins and planned to sell them." I bite my lip, then say softly, "The salon was here before the spa."

Travis jerks back at my words.

"Laura and Regina bought the building together. Laura and Walter...Eddie lived on this side of the duplex while Laura and Regina worked on the other side."

"What are you talking about? Regina and Vicky bought the building together."

I shake my head. "No, I spent the summer scouring Daysville's newspapers, remember? There's an article about Regina and Laura opening the salon together and after Laura was murdered, Vicky approached Regina about opening a spa in Laura's old home. It's all there." I pause and then add, "Maybe Laura hid the coins in the wall and planned to take Eddie and leave town. Regina somehow found out about her plans and when Laura wouldn't tell her where the coins were, she killed her. Maybe she thought Laura gave her parents the coins for safekeeping so she went there to get them and when they wouldn't or couldn't give them to her, she...I let my voice trail off because Travis's face is bright red and his fists are clenched.

"Regina didn't do this, Autumn, and I'm going to prove it."

He brushes past me and storms out the door.

I go to call out to him when a blast of cold hits me and I drop to my knees. Another vision fills my mind and plays like a movie.

Laura and Regina are laughing in the salon. A photographer is taking their picture. He positions Laura by the wall and has a fan blowing her hair across her face. He shows Regina the picture and she claps her hands together. "It's gorgeous, Laura. I think we should put it on the wall right behind you. Don't you think?"

Laura laughs and shakes her head then takes in the picture. "The lighting does bring out the red highlights you added."

"Red is the best color, darling." Regina spins Laura around.

Her long locks fan out around her and she giggles. Then she hugs Regina and says, "I'm so glad you're my best friend. I wouldn't have been able to get through the past few months after Dean died without you." A tear falls down her cheek.

Regina wipes it away and says, "We'll get through this... together. Now, let's go buy a big frame for that picture because we're blowing that baby up and putting it on our wall."

Laura laughs and the two women leave the salon arm in arm.

I fall forward and gasp for air. When I finally catch my breath, I ask, "Are you trying to tell me Regina didn't kill you? How do you know? Your back was to the wall. You didn't see your killer. You accused her of loving Dean. Maybe she was going to use the coins so they could run away together."

Nothing.

"Laura, I need your help. I don't want to believe Regina did this any more than Travis or you do, but I have to follow the clues. She obviously has a thing for your husband. She helped him and never told you he was alive. You were friends. Business partners." I pause then mutter, "Possibly criminals?"

A cold blast of air hits my face and suddenly, Laura appears. Her face is etched with rage and she's inches from my nose. She points to the coins and shakes her head. "We didn't steal these. I found them, well, Wallie did." She smiles then says, "He was playing ball in the living room and swung his bat right into the wall." She sighs at the memory. "He came running to get me. I was doing laundry. When we came back into the room, the bag and coins were on the floor." She stares down at the floor. "Dean didn't have a life insurance policy. The salon was struggling. I made a new hole in Wallie's wall and hid them. I was going to sell the coins to a collector, but...well, you know."

Tears brim my eyes. "I'm sorry."

She nods then studies me. "Regina dated Dean long before I met him. I didn't know. He went off to college and they broke up. He and I met while I was waiting table in a little café close to the cosmetology school. It was love at first sight, at least for me." She smiles. "Regina was my best friend. I didn't know they dated until after Dean supposedly died." She frowns then continues, "I found a letter from her to Dean in one of his books. It was written after we moved here. She told him she still loved him, but she didn't want to lose me as a friend so she swore him to secrecy about their relationship." She pauses. "I was angry when I found them in the cabin. I don't blame her for helping him. I would have done the same thing if he'd told me. I know he was protecting me and Wallie."

I nod then ask, "Did you tell Regina about the coins?"

Laura nods again.

"Did you tell her where they were hidden?"

She shakes her head.

"So, it's possible Regina...I mean you said the salon was struggling. She was raising Travis."

"But I was going to use the money to save the salon. I told her that."

"Revenge maybe? You stole her man. Maybe she snapped. Then decided to try and find the money. When she couldn't, she goes after your parents thinking they have the coins." Saying these words makes my stomach hurt. This is Regina. She's the most selfless person I know, but everyone has their breaking point, right?

Laura glares at me then disappears.

Great, my theories are blowing up in my face. I sigh and glance down at the coins. Travis will be back for these eventually. I scoop them up and head down the hall to the office. I plop down in the squeaky office chair, enter the combination on the safe under the desk and throw the bag inside.

A muffled scream comes from down the hall.

"Laura?" I hurry back to the red room.

No ones there.

Another screech sounds. It's on the other side of the wall.

Laura appears in her shimmering form. "Hurry, he has Regina." She points to the salon and disappears.

21

I creep toward the entrance of the salon. It's dark. Only a sliver of light shines from down the hall. They must be in Regina's office. I pray he hasn't hurt her... whoever he is. I think I've narrowed it down, but I'm still not one hundred percent sure.

I try the salon door. It's open, so I slip in, then cringe when the bell rings. Shoot. I forgot about the bell.

"Who's there?"

I duck behind the receptionist's desk when footsteps pound down the hall.

"The bell's finicky. No one's here. Now, please, just let me go," Regina pleads. "I told you I don't know where the coins are."

Footsteps retreat back to the office.

I move around the desk and tiptoe onto the salon floor. Boots and hardwood are not a good combination.

"I can't let you go, Regina. You know too much." A gun cocks.

I scan the room for a weapon. My eyes land on the fire extinguisher. I yank it off the wall, as quietly as possible, pausing momentarily to listen for anyone coming down the hall.

Murmurs and crying come from the office. I tiptoe as fast as I can in boots down the hall. I peek in the room and see Regina sitting in her desk chair with her head bent down in defeat. Then I see the gun pressed against her skull and I rush forward hurling the fire extinguisher.

"Autumn, no!" Regina shouts.

The gun goes off.

22

I stare down at the heap of man on the floor. The fire extinguisher is lying beside him on the ground and his head has a gash on it. "Dave?"

He doesn't move, but I can see his chest rising and falling.

Regina rushes over to me. "Autumn, you crazy girl. What were you thinking?"

"He was going to kill you."

She shakes her head and tears begin to run down her face before she gasps and reaches for me. "You've been shot."

"Really?" I glance down then it hits me. My arm is on fire. Blood is gushing from my bicep and pooling on the floor.

"I think it's just a flesh wound, but we need to get you to the hospital."

"Are you okay?" I take in her pale face and shaky hands. She should still be in the hospital. Her blood transfusion was only a day ago.

"Oh, Autumn, you sweet thing. I'm fine." Regina snatches a towel from her desk and presses it to my wound.

Wow, bullet wounds hurt. I stare down at Dave. "Dave was way down on my suspect list. I was expecting to see..."

"Me?" Dean steps into the room with a gun in his hand.

Regina mutters something under her breath about him being a snake in sheep's wool or something like that, I'm feeling kind of lightheaded.

"Actually, yes or the Judge."

Dean snorts. "Goodie two-shoes Judge Holliday. You've obviously lost your sleuthing touch, Miss Fisher."

I narrow my eyes at him. "You stole the coins, didn't you?"

"Actually, Dave stole them first." He gestures with the gun to an unconscious Dave. "I overheard his conversation with a coin dealer. When I found out how much they were worth, I took them. Hid them in the wall in the living room next door. Dave was livid and accused Harold of taking them. Seems those brothers all had an obsession with rare things. Harold denied it, of course. They fought. Dave punched Harold, splitting open his eyebrow. Harold left in a huff. Dave made me follow him because Dave had been drinking. Ole Dave has a passion for gin and tonic not to mention gambling." He shakes his head. "When we finally caught up to Harold, he'd been in an accident."

Regina and I gasp.

Dean nods. "Yes, Harold killed Travis's parents. His head wound was bleeding so bad, it obstructed his vision. He swerved into Travis's parents' lane and well..."

Regina begins to sob next to me.

I lean into her since my hand is pressed to the towel on my arm, which is completely soaked with blood. I'm feeling kind of nauseous and sway a little. *Don't faint, Autumn.* I take a deep breath and say, "So, you covered it up and disappeared."

Dean smiles. "It was actually the perfect escape. I was planning to wait a couple of months so Dave wouldn't suspect me then I was going to pack up Laura and Wallie... Eddie and leave this awful blimp of a town."

I glare at him. If I weren't bleeding, I would knock him out. No one talks about my town like that.

"Dave took my clothes and blew up the car then gave me some cash to disappear. So, I did."

"What about Laura? Eddie?"

A look of sadness passes over Dean's face before he replaces it with a look of determination. "Dave would have killed me anyway. I had no choice."

"You always have a choice," I spat.

He clenches his jaw and glares at me. "It was a pleasure meeting you, Miss Fisher." He cocks the gun.

I think fast. "Wait, so why didn't you take the money and coins and leave town?"

Dean hesitates.

"If you're going to kill me, why not lay it all out for me? My sleuthing mind is begging to know."

He smirks. "Fine. Since you've been so kind to my son, I'll grant your last request."

I force a smile.

He relaxes and lowers the gun, slightly. "I hid out in Laura's family's cabin for a week. There were too many people comforting Laura after 'I died', always bringing food or flowers. Once the hoopla went away, I snuck in when Laura was in the salon. The coins were gone. I figured Laura found them, although I didn't know how. The hole looked freshly patched. I assume Wallie probably had something to do with it." He smiles. "That boy and his baseball bat. I could have sworn he would grow up to be a professional ballplayer." He pauses, lost in the memory of the past then clears his throat and says, "I spent the next few months sneaking in when the house was empty, which was challenging since Laura worked next door and Eddie and the sitter were there a lot. I tore the house apart, not literally, of course. Laura would have suspected something. I couldn't find them. The money Dave gave me ran out." He rubs the back of his neck. "I have a slight gambling problem too. Dave and I spent a lot of time at the casino in Villsboro. His parents cut him off and Harold and Charles wouldn't help him either so we were both up a creek without a paddle, so to speak."

"But Dave has his store. He can't be broke."

Dean laughs. "The bank will be foreclosing on the store any day now."

I frown then ask, "So, you killed your own wife. Shot her in the back. For a bunch of coins."

"Those coins were the key to my freedom and he wouldn't tell me where they were. I had no place to go. I was supposed to be dead. I couldn't disappear without that money." He pauses then mumbles, "I still can't disappear without it."

"And you killed her parents because you thought she gave them the coins?"

"Actually, I thought she hid them in something. Her parents took all her belongings to their house so I broke in to find them. Her dad caught me going through boxes in the basement so I shot him. When her mom came to check out the noise..." A look of guilt passes over his face.

I glare at him then ask, "What about Harold?"

The guilt fades and a smile replaces it. "Good ole Harold. He felt so guilty about the accident and wanted to come clean, but Dave had already covered it up. Dave didn't want to go to jail too so he threatened to destroy Harold's store and chess collection if Harold muttered a word. So, Harold kept quiet." Dean sighs and shakes his head. "When Eddie came to town, Harold became extremely paranoid. I asked Harold to hack into Eddie's accounts, erase his past, link the supplies for the bomb, the shooting, the rats, and the fire to him in order to make it look like Eddie was making everything up. That way if Eddie somehow found some sort of evidence to convict any of us, no one would believe him." He pauses. "I also thought maybe Eddie had the coins. I tried to scare him, even distract him away from his house long enough to try and find the coins. Setting his house on fire gave me time to search for it without anyone coming or going. I came up empty though."

"Did you kill Harold?"

Dean nods. "His paranoia got really bad. I convinced him he did all the awful things he confessed to in his note. I guess the crazy coot liked to journal his feelings so I told him to get it all out on paper. Even made him write it to his twin brother. Then I told him I could end his pain." He shrugs as if killing a man is no big deal. "I dumped the bottle of sleeping pills into some whiskey and told him it would help him relax and forget everything." He smirks. "The guy chugged it down and well...you know."

Suddenly, the room turns ice cold and the lights flicker.

Dean points the gun at the lights. "What was that? Who's there?"

The lights go out and the room gets even colder. Laura appears flanked by three older shimmering ghosts, one is Harold and the other two, I'm guessing are her parents.

Dean's jaw drops. "Laura? Jane? Carson? Harold? H-h-how is this possible?"

They don't answer him as they swarm him like bees to a hive.

He shouts and screams then shots the gun at them. The bullets go straight through and hit the wall. Dean falls to the ground and continues screaming as the shimmery forms create some sort of cyclone around him.

Travis rushes into the room, gun out and ready to shoot. When he sees the scene in front of him, his jaw drops. "Wha-what's going on?"

The cyclone stops and disappears.

Dean's sitting on the floor with his arms around his knees, which are tucked into his chest. He's rocking back and forth, muttering to himself.

Travis blinks then averts his eyes over to me. He sees the blood-soaked towel and practically leaps over the desk. "What happened?"

I open my mouth to answer him when my vision blurs and everything goes black.

23

"Autumn? Autumn? Please, wake up"

I open my eyes and smile. "Hey."

Josh's blue eyes are filled with concern as he says something I don't hear.

"What?"

"I said, you're in the hospital. You lost a lot of blood. The bullet nipped an artery."

I glance down at my arm, which is in a sling. I groan. "How long before I can give a massage again?"

Josh chuckles and runs a hand over his scruffy chin. He's still in his clothes from the concert. "At least six weeks." He kisses the top of my hand, causing goosebumps to run up my arm and my heart rate picks up. The monitor's beep next to me. He glances up and raises an eyebrow at me.

I blush.

Someone clears their throat behind us.

I smile and say, "Hey, Eddie."

He steps up to the bed, wearing a dark suit and crisp white shirt and striped tie. "Hey, Autumn, how are you feeling?"

"Like someone shot me."

He smirks then frowns. "I'm sorry I put you in danger. If I had known…"

I shake my head. "None of this is your fault, Eddie. I knew the risks and I would do it again."

Josh growls beside me and squeezes my hand.

I squeeze it back then say to Eddie, "I'm sorry about your dad."

Eddie's brown eyes fill with tears. "Me too." He sighs. "I'll let you rest. I just wanted to check on you." He runs a hand through his brown hair. "Dave confessed to staging my fathe-Dean's death and paying him off. Dean fed him a bunch of lies and convinced him Regina stole his coins. Dean figured the only person left who Laura would trust with the coins would be Regina. He wanted to smoke her out, if she had them, without her seeing his true colors. Dean was planning to have Dave get the coins from Regina, then he was going to kill Dave, convince Regina to run away with him and disappear." He shakes his head and then continues, "Dave and Dean are going to jail for a long time and from the way Dean's acting, I'd say he's headed to a mental institution. Talking about ghosts forming some sort of tornado around him." Eddie shakes his head again.

I fight back a smirk. Obviously, Travis and Regina didn't set the record straight so I'm keeping my lips sealed too. "And Regina?"

Eddie sighs. "She's livid. Obviously, she feels betrayed. Dean lied to her for years. Convinced her to stage her own death to fool, essentially him, since he was making Harold send her threatening texts."

"Why would he do that?"

"To get her out of the salon so he could search for those coins."

I sigh. "Will she go to jail for helping him?"

Eddie runs a hand through his hair. "Judge Holliday and I are working with her attorney. She'll probably get some community service, but we haven't worked out the details yet."

I nod.

Eddie smiles at me and says, "I'll let you rest." He pats my leg. "Get well soon, Autumn, and thank you again."

I smile and watch him head to the door. The room suddenly goes cold. Laura appears with her parents in the doorway.

Eddie staggers back.

Laura reaches out and touches his cheek. "My sweet Wallie. I'm so proud of you. I love you so much."

"Mom? Grandpa? Grandma?"

They all nod then blow him a kiss and disappear.

Eddie stands there for a moment then glances over his shoulder and mouths, "Thank you" before heading out, shaking his head.

I wipe a tear from my cheek and focus on Josh, who is blinking like he's never seen a ghost before. I squeeze his hand again and he snaps out of it.

He squeezes my hand back and says, "Don't ever scare me like that again, Autumn. Promise me you won't go on any more cases without me."

"So, you're not going to make me promise to quit sleuthing?"

He snorts. "I wish I could, but it's a part of you so I can't ask you to give it up."

I blush and my heart kicks up again. Sheesh, maybe I should have the doctor check out my heart. I sigh and scan the room.

As if he can read my thoughts (I really feel like he can

sometimes), he says, "Travis stopped by earlier. He told me to text him when you woke up. He's swamped at the station and with helping Regina get out of her impending charges."

I frown.

"Autumn."

I force a smile. "It's fine. He's busy, not to mention he's moved on with Allison. He doesn't owe me anything."

"I told him the truth, Autumn."

I cringe. "Why?"

"Because I don't want you to have to choose me because of some silly lie."

"Have to choose you? What do you mean?"

"I mean..." Josh looks down at our intertwined hands. "Nothing. You need to rest. We can talk about this another time."

I tip his chin up so he's looking at me. "I'll always choose you, no matter what. You're my best friend."

"What if I want to be more?" His words come out so quietly, I almost don't hear them.

I suck in air and my heart takes off again, causing more beeping on the monitors. I'm not sure what to say. This is Josh. My best friend. My partner in crime. I've never thought of him as anything more than a friend...until recently. "Can I think about it?"

He smiles and squeezes my hand. "Of course. There's no rush." He lowers his voice and says, "I'd wait an eternity for you."

My heart flutters more and the monitors go crazy.

Josh laughs. "Let's change the subject before the nurses come in here and kick me out for working you up." He winks at me. "Pizza?"

I grin. "Always."

The End

A NOTE FROM THE AUTHOR

Thank you so much for reading, "Reflexology & Revenge"!! I so appreciate your support. This book was more of a challenge to write because it was a cold case. Trying to come up with suspects and motives for a thirty-something-year-old case is hard. I almost made Regina and Dean a modern-day Bonnie and Clyde, but I love Regina and don't want her sitting in jail when she can be stirring up trouble in Daysville. If you enjoyed this book, please consider leaving a review at the end. I love reading them. Whether they're good or bad, they make me a better writer, so thank you for taking the time to leave one.

Stay tuned for "Facials & Fugitives" coming out in October. Remember Maggie and her skittish behavior? Well, there's a reason for it and of course, who else would she turn to then Autumn?

Writing a book is a commitment and not something that

can be done alone. I have a few people to thank for helping with this book.

Mariah Sinclair is the queen of Cozy Mystery Covers and I absolutely adore this cover. Her work is incredible and I'm so thankful for her creative vision on this cover.

I would also like to thank Kate Farlow from Y'all That Graphic for the awesome pre-launch social media posts. If you haven't seen them, definitely check out my social media pages.

A huge shout out to Kelly H. for being my eyes on this book. She helped me spot plot holes, punctuation errors and made sure this book was flawless for you to enjoy.

My family is also amazing. They are so supportive of my writing. They call out character names when I need one, bring me food and drinks when I'm busy typing away and encourage me to follow my dreams. Without them, I would struggle. They're my rocks and I love them dearly.

Another huge thank you to you, my reader, I so appreciate you and your support. If you would like to follow me on social media or check out my blog. Here are the links:

Sleuth Mama Website (Blog)
Facebook Instagram Twitter Pinterest
Until next time...

Happy Reading,
Jenn

ABOUT THE AUTHOR

Jenn Cowan is the author of several genres and has pen names under Jenna Richert and J.R. Cowan. When she's not writing you can find her in her massage office working on clients, cooking up a storm in her kitchen, hitting her yoga mat, singing and dancing with her hubby at a concert, cheering on the sidelines for her kiddos or cozied up by the fire reading a good book. She loves a good mystery and a happily ever after.

OTHER BOOKS BY THE AUTHOR:

~A Cozy Spa Mystery Series

Massage & Murder (Book 1)

Hot Stones & Homicides (Book 2)

~Angelica's Manor of Love Duet

Love at the Manor

Fate at the Manor

~Non-Fiction

Massage Basics: A Step by Step Guide to at Home Massage

Made in the USA
Lexington, KY
02 September 2018